RIGHT WHERE YOU LEFT ME

Right Where You Left Me

Calla Devlin

atheneum

NEW YORK LONDON TORONTO
SYDNEY NEW DELHI

atheneum

An imprint of Simon & Schuster Children's Publishing Division
1230 Avenue of the Americas, New York, New York 10020

For information about special discounts for bulk purchases, please
contact Simon & Schuster Special Sales at 1-866-506-1949 or
business@simonandschuster.com.

The Simon & Schuster Speakers Bureau can bring authors to your
liveevent. For more information or to book an event, contact the Simon
& Schuster Speakers Bureau at 1-866-248-3049 or visit our website
at www.simonspeakers.com.

The text for this book was set in Centennial LT Std.

Manufactured in the United States of America

First Edition

10 9 8 7 6 5 4 3 2 1

Library of Congress Cataloging-in-Publication Data
Names: Devlin, Calla, author.
Title: Right where you left me / Calla Devlin.
Description: First Edition. | New York : Atheneum Books for Young Readers,
[2017] | Summary: When seventeen-year-old Charlotte Lang's father is taken
hostage while reporting on the aftermath of an earthquake in Ukraine,
Charlotte, a photographer most comfortable observing life, and her mother,
a reserved Russian immigrant who expresses caring through pastries, must
repair their strained relationship and find a way to rescue Charlotte's dad.
Identifiers: LCCN 2016052122
ISBN 9781481486996
ISBN 9781481487016 (eBook)
Subjects: | CYAC: Hostages—Fiction. | Kidnapping—Fiction. | Mothers
and daughters—Fiction. | Photography—Fiction. | Journalism—Fiction. |
Newspapers—Fiction. | Russian Americans—Fiction.
Classification: LCC PZ7.1.D488 Ri 2017 | DDC [Fic]—dc23
LC record available at https://lccn.loc.gov/2016052122

For my daughters, Lulu and Tillie

One

My father specializes in devastation. Not coups and wars— intentional and systematic—but nature's acts of violence, random and indiscriminate, destroying regions on a whim. Tsunamis, hurricanes, and earthquakes.

The muted TV broadcasts images of rubble and tears. An anchorwoman with enormous hair wrinkles her brow and mouths something heartbreaking. Death tolls and numbers of the missing. Dad will fly into the eye of the storm.

When I come home from school, I find him folding sweaters and thick socks, stacking them neatly into his duffel bag. Clothes intended for cold weather. He aligns the hems of a pair of jeans, long enough to fit his six-three frame. His height makes almost everything look miniature in comparison, furniture and ceilings more suited for a dollhouse. I drop my backpack to the floor, and when he walks over for a hug, he doesn't make me feel small at all.

"What happened?" I ask.

"Earthquake in Ukraine. I'm flying into Luhansk. Want to come with me to the airport?"

I glance at the TV, at the smoke billowing from what used to be an apartment or office building. Twenty-odd stories now pancake-flat. "Aftershocks?" I've become an armchair meteorologist.

"One so far. Worse than the quake."

Dad writes stories that make people weep from guilt and pity. Profiles of Mother Nature's refugees. The Red Cross's favorite journalist. When I pick up his passport and press credentials—JEREMIAH LANG, REPORTER, SAN FRANCISCO TRIBUNE—I want to toss them in the trash or hurl them off the Golden Gate Bridge. Anything to keep him here.

We head to the car. It's our routine: He drives to the international terminal and I drive myself home, keeping his car until his return. A temporary ownership, freedom that doesn't really make up for his absence. At least I'll have the car for my sleepover tonight at Emma's. He's a distracted driver, restless, tapping his foot and messing with the stereo. He becomes obsessed with different kinds of music: jazz, Icelandic pop, Puccini, Amy Winehouse. He researches and reads and downloads, forcing me to listen, lecturing me about the legacy of Etta James and the enduring power of *La Bohème*.

My mom says he is more of a teenager than I am. She means this as a compliment.

We listen to this Cuban hip-hop band that I liked at first but now makes my ears bleed from repetition. If I didn't love him so much, I'd delete the album from his library. He tells me about the dichotomy that is Cuba, about his recent trip to Havana to do an anniversary piece, of seeing police on every corner. Dad, a baritone storyteller, should work in radio. I am his dedicated audience, listening to details until I feel like his fellow traveler. It's been ten years since Hurricane What's-his-name paid a furious visit, but you couldn't tell now. All Cubans have housing and education and health care. The government values the arts, funding musicians and painters who promote its agenda and locking up those who don't. Bookstores are state-run, peddling propaganda and nothing more.

"I drank in Hemingway's favorite bar, but I couldn't buy one of his books," he says. "Hemingway loved Cuba. He had a house there. It's a museum now. I can't wait to take you there, Charlotte."

"I'll add it to the safe list." I feel compelled to travel to the countries he's visited and document the rebuilding and healing. I'd blow through rolls of film and fill up all the space in my phone with photos. It's selfish, but I need to replace the images in my head, the ones of orphans and widows and ruin. Thailand, Haiti, Nepal, and Ecuador. Now Ukraine.

Havana meets both of our criteria. Dad has enough airline miles for us to fly anywhere at least ten times over. But my parents prefer to take me to what they regard as safer places: Montreal, Oaxaca, Venice.

I'm not sure how they define "safe."

Mom's pushing for an Alaskan cruise. She wants me to see snow, but not in her homeland. Too many memories. Too much grief.

He taps the steering wheel to the rhythm. I look out the window, at the concrete and stucco landscape. I pull my camera from my backpack and take the cap off the lens. I started doing this a couple of years ago, taking a good-bye picture each time he leaves. When I get home, I'll print it out and tape it to the fridge. "Did Mom give you a list?" I ask.

"She wanted me to bring a second suitcase." He smiles when he says this.

They met when he had just started at the newspaper. His editor sent him to St. Petersburg to cover the flooded Neva River. Out of the entire newsroom, Dad was the only one remotely familiar with Russia—he'd taken a class on Russian lit and knew a handful of useless phrases. Apparently, Tolstoy is responsible for his career.

Mom, just finishing college, was his translator. She still pines for her favorite lotion and tea from home, brands too obscure to buy online.

"Your mom said to tell you she'll be home late tomorrow night, after her cooking class," he says. "I made a lasagna for you guys. I should be back in a week. Maybe earlier."

Mom is a baker, and Dad loves to cook. Dad travels the world, but Mom is more absent. I'm an only child, accustomed to being alone in the house, wandering the halls like a ghost. Sometimes I like it this way.

But not today.

We exit the freeway, and I want him to drive at a snail's pace, inching along at five miles per hour. I'll endure more of his hip-hop. I'll ask more questions about Cuba and Ukraine. I'll recite trivia about extreme weather. I'll promise to go to Dad's alma mater, NYU, even though I won't know if I got in for a few weeks, even though I really want to stay home and go to Berkeley. I'll even speak Mom's Russian.

I spot the airport, magnificent with its glass facade and dangling vines, and I want him to slam on the brakes. I don't want him to leave. I don't want to spend the week alone in a silent house with my mother. But I don't tell him this. I don't say, *Stay.* I've inherited Mom's light blue eyes and reserve, so I just reach for his hand until we idle in front of a skycap.

"I'll be back in a few days, kiddo."

"I'll be here," I say. "Right where you left me."

He kisses my cheek. I tell him I love him. Before I climb

into the driver's seat, I snap his picture. He gives me his usual over-the-top grin. I watch him carry his duffel bag through the doors, beneath the DEPARTURES sign, until he disappears into a crowd of tourists.

I don't leave until an airport cop pats the hood of the car and waves me away.

Two

Dad is a bridge between my mom and me. A conduit, nearly electric in intensity, drawing us together. Without him, we circle around each other, two planets suddenly out of orbit.

Even though I'm tired from staying up way too late at Emma's, and wiped from an essay test in English, I wait up long past dinner, watching the earthquake coverage and refreshing a couple of news sites, but she doesn't come home until late, too late for me to stay up. My friends, all on the school newspaper, stay up with me, texting details we see on TV, searching for a glimpse of Dad.

It's too late to call them, especially on a weeknight, even though we're awake, texting so fast that I almost can't keep up.

I want to text Josh, who's also on the paper, but we've never texted before. Five days ago, he kissed me. For the first time. Hopefully not the last. Only earthquakes could preoccupy me more than Josh. I don't have his number.

I'm a huge fangirl of this one news anchor who wears frosty pink lipstick and matching dresses. She reads the teleprompter like she means every word. She's tender but strong. I think she's perfect. My friends disagree, describing her as sentimental and a bad dresser. They can be a little judgmental.

I wake early to sounds in the kitchen. *"Dobroye utro,"* Mom says. Good morning. She offers me a distracted smile, which, with her asymmetrical eyes, a leftover from her stroke, creates the illusion that she's winking. Years of yoga got rid of her limp, but there's nothing she can do about her face.

She's disfigured from giving birth to me. I swear I was born into this world feeling guilty for hurting her, even if I didn't mean to. Even if it was out of my control.

Nature can be cruel to the earth and to the body.

She's been up for hours, cooking downstairs until Nadine, who owns the bakery, arrives to open the store. They're kindred, Mom and Nadine. Both from St. Petersburg. Both baking prodigies. Both preferring quiet over conversation. My parents moved into the flat before I was born. Mom started helping downstairs out of homesickness and grief, restless with a newborn, in desperate need of company. Over time, my parents bought the apartment and Mom took on more responsibility at the bakery. She'll buy it whenever Nadine is ready to pass it down. I used to bake with them more, before I joined the paper and the cross-country team. Now I'm there only on Saturdays, Nadine's day off. It feels like a family business.

If I cared about flour, sugar, and butter more than running and photography, maybe we'd be kindred too. I share the same serious streak. Mom says it's because we're Russian. I have an old soul. I'm self-contained. Dad thinks I'm serious because I'm an only child, a mini-adult. Maybe we'd be a normal family if my sister had lived, the two of us playing and screeching and fighting like other kids.

When I was in first grade, I dumped a bag of flour over my head, a dusty ghost hoping for a laugh, anything to bring out that goofy smile I know Mom lets loose once in a while. And she did. She helped me clean up, and we spent the day baking. She sounded giddy when she relayed the story to Dad and then, later, Nadine. But the next day, we returned to our serious silence.

Even though she's only fifteen years older than Mom, Nadine is like my grandmother. When I was little, I called her Babushka. When she turned fifty-five, Nadine made me stop, saying it made her feel too old. I call her Tatya Nadine now, aunt. Still, she mothers us, Mom the most.

Flour dusts Mom's shirt, and she smells of chocolate and baked apples and sugar. I want to bottle the scent and carry it with me.

"How was last night?" I don't ask what time she finally came home from teaching her cooking class at the cultural center. I don't insist that she have a curfew until Dad returns, even though I want to.

She gives me this look, one I'm used to. It's like she knows my face but not my name—like I'm an acquaintance she hasn't seen in a while. I want to say, *Hi, it's me, Charlotte. Remember? You gave birth to me seventeen years ago.* I don't have a clue what's in her head.

"Khoroshiy." Nice. "We had a good group of people for a Wednesday. Almost a dozen."

A loaf of bread, fresh from the oven downstairs, steams on the counter. I reach for it and begin to rip off a piece.

"Stop, Charlotte," Mom says, reaching for a knife. I should know better. It's bad luck to tear bread with your hands—you must use a knife. If you don't, something awful will happen, so bad that your life will be broken. Mom's not normally so superstitious, but whenever Dad's away, she follows all of her old-world customs. There are too many for me to remember, especially when I haven't had coffee.

"There's sesame roll in the oven," she says as she slices me a piece of bread.

"Do you have anything going on tonight?" I ask, brushing the hair out of my face.

"Nadine and I need to go shopping. I'll bring you home

some mu shu pork. *Vash lyubimyy.*" Your favorite.

She says this with her back to me, busy peeling a pear over the sink.

"Have you heard from Dad?" I ask. "I put his good-bye picture on the fridge."

There. She turns around. Now she looks at me—really looks at me—and shakes her head. "It's too soon. The power and cell towers are still down. Maybe one of the TV reporters will loan him a phone." She walks over and smiles at the photo. "That's a good one."

Dad writes about the aftermath of disasters, taking backseat to the breaking-news reporters who haul generators across oceans. He stays after they broadcast their flurry of initial coverage. Dad's articles remind us that tragedy lasts longer than a news cycle. Some people call his work fluffy and sentimental. I want to push them into an active volcano.

"Will you text me when you hear from him?" I ask.

She must hear the worry in my voice because she smiles softly. "Of course," she says with a nod. She's graceful but precise in her movements, something she learned from studying dance. Mom always looks pretty, even wearing an apron and sweaty from a hot kitchen. Her hair's in a high ponytail, and it makes her look younger, more like one of the grad students at the nearby college. She slides the peeled pear across the counter. "Eat, Charlotte. You don't want to be late for school."

We settle into yet another spell of silence. It hangs around us like wallpaper. As I pour a cup of coffee, I'm overcome with the urge to howl or yodel or scream—anything to fill the room with noise. I miss Dad, who barrels through the apartment, insisting we listen to public radio or music or passages from news articles or awful jokes and puns.

"I better shower," I say, leaving the room so quickly that my coffee almost sloshes over the mug's brim.

When I reemerge dry and dressed, Mom's gone. She left some sesame roll, warm as I take a bite. On a sticky note, she wrote, *Have a good day at school.* I fold it in half and slip it into my pocket.

A squirrel performs a high-wire act on one of the slim branches of our giant spruce tree. I think we meet eyes for the briefest moment, and I convince myself it's Mom in animal form. A game I play: casting my family as various Russian folktale characters, people and spirits from books Mom read aloud to me when I was in elementary school.

She is Samovila, the elusive, shape-shifting forest goddess, who might visit a normal human—if they're lucky. If they interest her. If she has some free time. She might share her magical gifts. Might. Only if she deems them worthy to listen to her stories and share her secrets.

I turn around before the squirrel runs away.

* * *

When I climb into Dad's car, it's too easy to imagine what could go wrong: a head-on collision, running over a bicyclist, some other catastrophe. I'm not a paranoid person—the opposite, actually—but the hours following Dad's departures are always filled with the awareness of how everything can change in an instant.

Continental plates collide, wildfires consume, tsunamis swallow.

Sisters don't wake up from naps.

School is my antidote. Boredom and monotony have a way of killing my perspective. I distract myself with more important things, like crappy quiz scores, college acceptance/rejection anxiety, and how my locker neighbor is hoarding large volumes of candy.

I hear Emma before I see her, the tumble of books and subsequent profanity announcing her arrival. Chaos follows her like a loyal dog.

I don't bother racing to her aid. At least one or two boys will scramble to pick up her stuff. I'm equally cute, or so I'm told, but Emma's goofy, her clumsiness more slapstick and endearing. Dad says I hide behind my camera too much. If I'm going to be a journalist like him, I need to ask more questions. I need to see the whole story and not just the shot.

Emma's hair is stacked high on her head, a messy bun

that somehow looks perfect. With her long, wavy red hair, she looks like she stepped out of a Botticelli painting. Her mom must be on a business trip because Emma's wearing a pair of ripped jeans and an almost sheer T-shirt—clothes, according to her mother, meant for the weekend, not for school.

Her parents keep a spotless house. They're minimalists, appreciating what they call "clean lines," which means bare walls and expensive brown furniture. It's the kind of house you see in magazines. I think it's stark and cold. Sitting in the living room feels like wearing a pair of stilettos, shoes that force you to walk slowly and with caution.

I call Emma's house "the bunker." Brushed concrete walls and vaulted ceilings. It seems safe in the event of nuclear war or zombie apocalypse.

Mom hates it because it reminds her of the Soviet Union, that utilitarian architecture she says was designed to house the masses.

Unlike their severe decorating style, Emma's parents are warm and generous. They let her and her brother decorate their rooms to their liking. Mr. and Mrs. Archer impose two rules: Dirty clothes belong in the hamper—not on the floor—and food must be disposed of on a daily basis. No rotting pizza or moldy Girl Scout cookies. Thin Mints spoil with remarkable speed.

"I'm starving," Emma says. "I've been living on Pop-Tarts and takeout. Oh, and I got a C-plus on my stupid chemistry exam."

"That's still better than last time," I say. Emma nails anything that involves words, but when it comes to numbers or labs, she gets paralyzed. She has the most lopsided SAT scores on the planet—near perfect in verbal, bottom tenth percentile in math. Right now, the periodic table is killing her. She waits till the last minute no matter how hard we try to get her to start early. Her parents won't find out unless she gets a D. If they did, they'd hire an army of tutors and we'd never see Emma again. We won't let that happen.

We carry our trays of barely edible food toward the spot in the cafeteria claimed for the Editorial Roundtable, the name we gave ourselves, "we" being those of us who run the school newspaper. We're exclusive and terrifying. We have the power to publish an unflattering photo or elevate someone's social status with a single story.

Emma is the editor and proofreader. Everyone defers to her. Isaac writes what he regards as hard news and investigative pieces. He's obsessed with CNN and the *New York Times*. He is equal parts ruthless and reverential. I am the photo editor. Everyone smiles for me. Megan is our adviser. Our school, a masterful example of bureaucracy, frowns upon the use of first names. Technically, she is Miss Eng, but she just got out of the Peace Corps and this is her first teaching job. She describes herself as our peer and a socialist. We adore her. Josh does the layout, videos, and web page. He doesn't eat with us. He barely talks to us, but he is brilliant with anything visual.

I know he likes me, but my friends might be another story. They rejected him a while ago.

Josh defies categorization. He doesn't wear a trench coat, but he talks to guys who do. He lives on the computer, but he isn't the math programming type or a gamer. He talks about film and art and design. He bikes everywhere but isn't a jock. He has friends, but he doesn't stick to one group. It's like he owns the school, an eccentric, weirdo king who floats from crowd to crowd, all happy to have his attention. But he's not popular in the class president or homecoming king sense. He's the perfect definition of "charismatic."

He's been suspended twice, and everyone says that he's flirting with expulsion. One time, he put cameras in the hallways and posted various videos of what he called "douche moves." Basically, bullying and typical jerk behavior, daily occurrences at our school. Stuff like Matt Cavanaugh grabbing Sonia Ortiz's butt or mean girls being mean girls or Danny King, pre–anger management counseling, hitting or shoving or yelling at anyone who stands in his path.

To protect the innocent, Josh said, he blurred out the

victims' faces and then did these crazy voice-overs. Everyone knew it was him, but Josh refused to stop broadcasting his daily dispatches. As soon as the school took down a camera, he hid a new one. The only way to make him stop was to kick him out of school.

He retaliated by editing the footage and entering it in a short-film contest. He won third place.

No one knows the details of his second suspension. He refuses to share them, which drives Emma and Isaac crazy.

Josh dresses like a bike messenger and rides with the Critical Mass people who shut down the city on a monthly basis, claiming the streets for cyclists, blocking traffic and intersections. He's political in a more vigilante sense, but he doesn't have a cause. I've never heard him preach about the perils of climate change or the benefits of a vegan diet. The paper is his only extracurricular activity—that I know of.

I have been almost in love with him since sophomore year. I've studied everything about him without crossing the stalker line. I've stored up desire like a woodland animal preparing for winter. Last week, we took the same spring break camp. Five days and four nights on the Berkeley campus. Hours full of classes and lectures on multimedia art. He studied film and web design while I immersed myself in photography, learning more digital techniques. We didn't know anyone else, so we gravitated to each other. I would have gravitated anyway. He's my magnet, a forceful and unwavering pull. We ate together. We talked about more than school. And we kissed.

If it hadn't been sunrise, and if we hadn't been sober, hopped up on caffeine, I would doubt it even happened. Except I swear I can still feel his lips behind my ear, on that swirl of hair at the base of my neck. And his fingers, first on my collarbone and then down the length of my spine. And his mouth, the taste of coffee and half-and-half and a uniquely Josh flavor, salty with a hint of sweet. Kind of like black licorice.

I saw him once today, at the other end of the hall. I caught him staring, but someone started talking to him as soon as I met his eyes.

Isaac thinks Josh has a personality disorder. Emma thinks he's arrogant. Even a little creepy. Maybe even dangerous. They tease me enough to make it clear that they don't understand—or approve.

They see delinquent.

I see curious.

They see full of himself.

I see confidence.

Emma agrees, however, that he is oddly attractive. According to her, it's his only redeeming quality.

Again, my friends can be a little judgmental.

As soon as I reach our table, I search the room for him. A treasure hunt. Josh doesn't have a usual spot. Today, he sits seven tables away. His dark hair, a little on the longer side, falls into his face so I can't see his eyes.

Isaac is in the middle of one of his tall tales. For someone who strives for objective journalism, he's prone to hyperbole. Especially when he's trying to impress Megan, who never appears in the cafeteria. He almost knocks over my tray with his bird-in-flight inspired gestures. Isaac speaks with more than his hands. Conversation is a full-body experience.

"Sorry, Charlotte, I'm trying to explain how huge that quake is. Crazy."

"At least the aftershocks are over." I pull out my phone to check for texts or missed calls from Dad. Nothing.

"Charlotte," Isaac says. "Look." He hands me his phone. Another quake hit an hour ago. This one larger than the first.

A huge aftershock, and we still haven't heard from Dad. I feel like I have a rattlesnake in my belly, knotting and unknotting itself. I try really hard not to panic because, as Mom reassured me just this morning, it's too soon to be worried. But he usually sends a text or email by now, one or two words, maybe even a sentence, letting us know that he's safe. Nothing this time.

I don't say anything as I place Isaac's phone back in his hand. I type on mine, which looks and feels a decade older than Isaac's, a hand-me-down from Mom. First, I go to the *San Francisco Tribune* website and scroll down the page. Nothing on the quake except for some wire photos. Then I search for Dad's name, which pulls up his Havana anniversary story. Nothing from Ukraine.

"Derr`mo." My friends are used to my Russian profanity and have committed various curse words to memory. That comes in handy during class. Other kids speak Spanish and Cantonese, but there aren't a lot of Russians at my school.

I send Mom a quick text:

Anything from Dad?

I keep my phone on the table.

They're staring at me. "It always takes him a couple of days to file a story," I say.

"Want to watch the CNN video?" Isaac asks.

"Don't be such an asshat," Emma says. "Put your phone away and tell me how you're going to help me with my chem homework."

They banter about the molecular composition of gases as I watch my phone. By the time the bell rings, Mom still hasn't texted back.

In English class, all I can think about is Dad. I stare at my phone, waiting for it to light up with a text. I can't follow the lesson on the intricacies of Toni Morrison's lyrical prose. When someone hovers at my desk, I look up. Josh. All week,

I'd been worried that he'd be shy or embarrassed with me. That maybe he regretted our spring-break kiss. Regretted me. But when he smiles, I know that's not the case. Mr. Wright tells him to sit down, and as usual, as soon as class ends, Josh is the first one out the door. Like he's racing the bell.

After school, Emma and I walk through Golden Gate Park, dodging puddles and thick raindrops falling from the many eucalyptus and pine trees. Seagulls circle above as they scavenge for scraps. I glance up at the tops of the trees disappearing into the fog, dense and thick, making the underbrush look electric green in comparison.

We pass the Japanese Tea Garden and the Drum Bridge, a steep and intricate structure the shape of a perfect half circle. In the fog, it looks ancient, as though we stumbled through a time warp and emerged in an earlier century.

"Hang on a second, Em," I say, and pull out my camera. The lens mists over as soon as I remove the cap. That only adds to the effect. "Stop there."

Emma obliges and stands in front of the bridge. Wisps of red hair frame her face, and her indigo jacket pops against the misty gray.

"I can't believe you didn't take pictures all day," she says, knowing I like to have something to occupy me when I'm nervous. I'm not allowed to carry my camera at school—only when working on the paper or yearbook. I may have had an unfortunate incident documenting the Presidential Challenge in P.E. My gym teacher has yet to forgive me for her unofficial school portrait. Thank God she doesn't coach cross-country or I'd be running extra miles.

"I'm thinking of asking Megan for a permission slip so I can carry my camera around. You know, say I'm 'documenting student life' or some crap like that."

When Emma nods, I ask her to be still as I snap a few shots. She's a natural model and runs through every imaginable expression and pose in rapid succession like an interpretive dancer. When she starts to fidget, I get the hint and put the camera away.

"I want you to know that out of respect for your dad, I'm not going to give you grief about Josh. Not today, anyway. But it's coming."

I raise an eyebrow at her. "Thanks for the warning."

When she smiles, it's easy to understand why almost everyone loves Emma. She returns to my side, and we keep walking along the path. I don't have a good reason to worry. So why can't I shake this feeling?

Right before the end of school, Mom had finally texted back.

Nichego. Nothing.

I don't want to panic. This has happened before. Power

is erratic. Phone lines and cell towers are down for days. An entire country can be immobilized. Japan, one of the most advanced nations in the world, was at a complete standstill after its last quake. It took days for Dad to file a story.

Emma understands when to talk and when to be quiet, the best kind of friend. We walk through the park because that's what I like to do when I'm feeling stressed. Emma knows this, so when she asked if she could drive Dad's car, I said yes, sure we'd end up here.

I finger the hair tie circling my wrist and focus on pulling my hair into a ponytail. "This feels different," I finally say. "He usually texts good night or good morning or something. Anything."

"Are all of the big papers running their own coverage?" she asks. Emma knows the difference between a paper having a reporter at the scene versus a paper that runs a wire story by the Associated Press.

Right after lunch, in biology, various parts of the brain had been listed on the chalkboard—the medulla oblongata, cerebrum, cerebellum, pineal body—and we were challenged to sort them according to function. Which controlled breathing? I couldn't focus. I didn't care if I got in trouble for blowing off the assignment. Hiding my phone, bent over like Quasimodo in the *Hunchback of Notre Dame,* I checked other news sites, everything from the big papers like the *New York*

Times to smaller citizen journalist blogs. I did the same thing during my last three classes. Social media made my head spin. Too much fragmented information.

"I checked," I say. "All of the major papers are running their own coverage. Dad is the only one who hasn't published."

She takes a deep breath and stops walking. "Just because the *Washington Post* is running something doesn't mean that anything happened to your dad. He doesn't write those short articles about the Richter scale."

"What if something did?" My voice is so soft, it competes with the breeze.

After a quiet moment, Emma says, "Your dad is Indiana Jones. He's going to be fine."

My phone buzzes. A text from Mom.

Idi domoy. Come home.

Three

Uncle Miguel is such a regular fixture in our apartment that it feels perfectly normal to find him in his favorite chair. Only today, Dad isn't sitting across from him drinking the cheap Mexican beer they love, playing cards, and debating the details of Central American coups d'état. Today, he looks tired, more tired than usual, and when I step forward, I see that he hasn't shaved or even showered and that his clothes are all rumpled.

He looks like Dad after a long flight home, after spending days without running water and electricity. He has that same look too, the one Dad has when he mentions how many people died in a disaster. Dad normally doesn't talk about that, but sometimes he can't help it and something slips out.

Mom steps into the room carrying a plate of sesame roll and offers Uncle Miguel a piece.

"Thanks, Valentina," he says.

She gives him a weak smile. When she turns to me, I see her eyes, red-rimmed, and how her eyeliner is so smudged that she looks bruised.

I want her to say something, but she doesn't. I'm startled when she puts down the plate and wraps her arms around me, briefly. My fingers feel so cold, it's like I have frostbite, but I still hold on to her, almost squeezing.

No one speaks. They know something, clearly, but they look at each other, at their hands, at everything in the room but me. That's when I collapse on the couch and close my eyes. That's when I know something terrible is happening.

"Skazhite mne," I say. Tell me. *"Pozhaluysta."* Please.

Uncle Miguel, kind, portly Uncle Miguel, my godfather, Dad's boss, his best friend from college. He is the one who finally tells me my father is missing.

"Lottie, the last time we heard from your dad, he was finishing up his story and driving to one of the rural areas. He was with a photographer and another reporter from France. Then the last aftershock hit. There was a big explosion, probably a gas line, that's blocking the roads. I'm sorry, honey, but no one has seen him since. We're doing everything we can. You know your dad—he's resourceful. He's probably at a camp passing out cigarettes and writing a bunch of profiles. We just can't get through to him."

It takes a minute for me to catch my breath and really

hear what Uncle Miguel is saying. They can't find Dad. Everything I've been feeling, all the worry and anxiety, is real. It was worse today than ever before, like somehow I knew something was wrong. My heart races, and I have to think to breathe, as though my body has stopped working. This can't be happening. Dad is too big and rambunctious for anyone to lose him.

"How do you know he's not hurt?" I ask. My voice comes out shaky from trying not to cry. I uncross my legs and put both feet on the hardwood floor, trying to ground myself any way possible.

"I'm sure he's fine," Uncle Miguel says. "It's chaos over there. We'll find him as soon as things calm down."

I'd be more likely to believe Uncle Miguel if he didn't look so wrecked. Mom squeezes my hand, and I don't let go. I look them each in the eye, register their obvious grief. "What else?" I ask. "There must be more because, Uncle Miguel, you look like you've been microwaved or something."

"They were in the area of the quake. Hundreds of people are missing. We're working with all of the rescue groups, but it's tough to get information."

The pictures are vivid in my mind: fire and dust and rubble. Mom squeezes my hand again. I close my eyes, just for a moment, and try to push away my fear.

Uncle Miguel pulls his laptop from his bag and turns it

so I can see the screen. He opens a map and traces the area with his finger, tapping the place where Dad was last seen.

"This village was hit hard," he says. "Valentina, have you ever been anywhere near there?"

Mom shakes her head. "We never visited Ukraine. I don't have family there."

When Uncle Miguel closes the map, I see a photo of a car belly-up on the side of the road.

"What's that?" I ask, my heart picking up speed.

He shuts his computer a little too quickly. "The photographer sent a few pictures."

"Wait." I try to even my breathing a little, suck in some air. "I thought you said you haven't heard from them?"

"The photographer's local," he says with his eyes glued to the computer. "A freelancer from Kiev. He showed up at a camp and said he doesn't know where your dad and Pascal, the French reporter, are."

"Isn't that weird? Mom, isn't it?"

She smooths my ponytail, a memory of a touch, and I feel like I'm little again. "That's the problem, *moy rebenov*, it is and he won't tell us more." My child. She hasn't referred to me like that since I was in kindergarten.

"We're doing everything we can to get Jerry home," Uncle Miguel says, sitting as straight as his beer belly allows.

When I lean against Mom, she doesn't stiffen or make

an excuse to return to the kitchen. She stays, something I've never needed like I do now. She cuts me a piece of sesame roll even though I can't think of food without wanting to puke.

I look at my hands and see that I've clenched my fists without noticing. I'm old enough to understand that Uncle Miguel is offering a promise that he can't keep. It's a wish and a vow, but he isn't in Ukraine. He can't control the weather. He can't call in the National Guard for a manhunt.

"Will you stay?" I ask. "For a while?"

We both know that I adore him, but right now, he's Dad's proxy, my only connection to him, the closest thing to having my family in one place.

Four

Way before I joined the school newspaper, Dad taught me the essential questions reporters ask. A story is incomplete until all are answered and supported. I know Uncle Miguel won't sleep until he gets answers. He's as determined as Dad—and as stubborn.

He'll work twenty-four hours straight if necessary, until he finds Dad and figures out how to get him home. I should be reassured by this, but I'm not. I trust Uncle Miguel. He's like family, and I know he'll do anything within his power to find my father. Still, I can't help but wonder if that will be enough.

How, from his office on Market Street, can he answer these questions:

Who knows where Dad is?

What exactly happened to him?

Where is he?

Why can't they find him?

When did he last make contact with other reporters?

How can we find out if he's safe? If he's alive? If he'll come home?

I want to grab my camera and a notepad and my passport and drive to the airport now. I may be kind of shy and introverted, but I'm as stubborn and determined as both Dad and Uncle Miguel. And I speak Russian.

Nothing—NOTHING—is worse than feeling helpless. That's exactly how I felt as soon as Uncle Miguel's words reached my ears. It's like all of the gravity on Earth vanished along with Dad, and I'm floating through space without anything holding me down. Like something weightless. Like I'm nothing.

I take stock of my normally neat room. Things have their place, and usually it's comforting to put clothes in drawers and books on shelves. None of that matters now. I pick up a pair of jeans, but drop them on the floor again. I don't have the energy to care.

Emma's closet bulges with clothes and shoes while mine is full of photo albums and boxes of pictures, each labeled with names, locations, and dates. I'm an archivist as well as a photographer. I pull down a recent box, family pictures from Christmas and our last big vacation in Italy. The back of my bedroom door is empty, the only blank surface in my room. I begin to cover it with images of Dad wearing a Santa hat, Dad hiking in the redwoods, Dad standing at the rail on our boat ride to Capri, the wind blowing back his hair. Squinting into the sun. He looks happy and free. That's how I want to imagine him now.

Maybe Uncle Miguel's right: Dad is probably sitting in some camp waiting for cell phone service to be restored. Maybe he's teaching the locals how to play five-card draw. He believes poker is the universal card game. Plus, people drink and smoke when they play cards, which means they speak more freely. They share stories. Even secrets. An effective way to get answers.

I allow myself to imagine him there, really picture where he could be. It must be a fallen building or blocked road keeping him from us. Dad can handle people. He can talk his way out of almost anything. He must be trapped somewhere, because his quasi-giant stature means he can climb and jump from atypical heights. He's in decent shape, and he even ran that 5K with me last year. I bet he could still run a mile without stopping.

Most importantly: Dad is fearless. If he's trapped somewhere, he will find a way out. I have to believe that. I know deep inside that he'll do whatever he can to come home. He knows we love him. We're waiting for him. Mom and I can't live without him.

I try to remind myself of Dad's strength and quick reflexes and street smarts, but it's not enough to ease the tension in my muscles or knots in my belly. No matter how much I list the many reasons he's probably safe, my anxiety builds. Something's wrong. I know it.

After I was born, Mom was too sick to hold me for longer than a few minutes at a time. Dad was the one who cradled me for hours, letting me nap on his chest. Ever since I was little, I've felt that invisible bond, that connection. I pick up a snapshot and stare at his face, well aware that he's never felt farther away than he does right now.

Five

Zero period: the hour before school officially starts, the hour devoted to extracurriculars and extra credit and extra help for those who need it. For us, it means the first of two periods of working on the newspaper. One hundred minutes of freedom. Just us and Megan and the news.

When we returned from summer vacation, we found Megan in the classroom, smiling like someone who arrived early to see a movie and scored the best seat in the theater. We knew Mr. McGuire was retiring, and we'd spent break guessing who would take over the newspaper. We'd braced ourselves for one of the English teachers, none as good as our ancient Mr. McGuire. We never expected someone new and so young.

Megan brought in a secondhand coffeemaker and brews extra-strong French roast. She talks about how a free media is an essential component of democracy. How everyone should have equal access to quality news. How journalists are as necessary as doctors. She'd heard of Dad and was full of praise.

I like her because she's worldly—second generation like me. Emma likes her because she's passionate. Isaac likes her because of the short (*short*) dress she wore that first day of school. I suspect Josh likes her because she doesn't force him to interact with us like Mr. McGuire did.

She greets us every morning with coffee and newspapers to scan from beginning to end. She wants us to feel the newsprint between our fingers. She spares us the classifieds.

I come early. The room doesn't welcome me with the usual smell of coffee, but Megan looks up with a smile. I pretend I am her favorite. I've thought about copying her bobbed jet-black hair, but my curls would never cooperate. Silver hoops line her ears from tip to lobe. Despite the March rain, she's wearing a vintage sundress that reveals her sleeve of botanical tattoos.

"Getting a head start?" she asks.

I spent all night awake in bed hoping for a text from Dad. I wanted to come to school at four a.m. At five. I settled for six thirty, a half hour before the first bell rings.

"My dad," I say. "They can't find him. He's officially missing."

"Sit," she says, and points to a chair. "You haven't heard from him at all?"

I shake my head. "He's *gone,* gone. Everyone's worried. My mom. His editor. He was in the middle of the quake, but I think there's more going on." I tell her about the French reporter and the mysterious photographer. I wonder if she notices that my hands are shaking. I hide them in my lap. "He sent in pictures, but he won't say anything about my dad. That makes no sense at all. He must've said something if he's working for them, right?"

Megan frowns and picks up a copy of Dad's paper, one of several fanned on the table. There it is, on the front page of the *Tribune,* a photo by Ivan Barno of helmeted men climbing a mountain of rubble. The caption says something about rescue workers searching for survivors.

"There could be an explanation," she says. "Maybe he was shooting pictures while your dad and the other reporter interviewed people. Then the earthquake happened and they got separated." She taps the paper. "Think of the chaos, Charlotte. Look at this."

"So my dad could be trapped inside a building? Then why wouldn't the photographer say that?" I'm tired and panicked and I want someone to tell me where the hell Dad is. I know Megan doesn't have this information, but she knows more about journalism and the world than I do.

She stands and gives me an arm hug. "We don't know what he said."

As soon as I feel her arm around me, I can't help the tears. I'm trying to be tough and composed. Dad would expect that of me. Mom needs me to be the stoic one, but I'm not strong enough. I'm scared, and all I want is to see a reassuring text from Dad.

"Listen," Megan says, "I understand why you're worried, but this sort of thing happens all the time. When I was in the Peace Corps, sometimes we couldn't get reception for days because that's how it goes in underdeveloped places. Ukraine's more advanced, but the earthquake did so much damage. I know you don't want to hear this, Charlotte, but you're going to have to be patient and try to stay positive. In this case, no news is good news, okay?"

I wipe my nose with my sleeve, then, embarrassed, roll it up to hide the smudge of snot. "Yeah," I say. "I'll try."

She hugs me tight before releasing me. I'm filled with helium again, untethered.

"Isaac will riot if he comes and the coffee's not ready," she says as she fills the pot with water.

Isaac is very serious about his caffeine. He drinks his coffee black because he thinks that's how all hardened newsmen take it. He's unbearable without it. We all cater to his addiction.

Ivan the Photographer's picture taunts me. It may be the last place where Dad was safe: that decimated building,

those heavy, loose bricks. I can't bear the idea of him standing near it—or inside—before the earth rippled beneath his
feet and the walls crashed down. He could have gotten out in
time. But then Ivan the Photographer would have seen him.

That's when it hits me, really hits me. Dad could be
trapped or worse. He may never come home.

Stay positive.

"Charlotte?" Hearing Megan's voice snaps me out of it. I
try to be discreet as I wipe my nose again.

"I have an idea," she says. "We're going to do some investigative journalism. Sit tight until the others get here."

I fiddle with my phone, taking a break from the news to
read my email and flip through recent pictures of Dad. The
door opens and I turn around hoping to see Emma, but it's
Josh.

He must see how absolutely messed up I am because
he freezes midstep and just looks at me, his smile disappearing and his brow furrowing. He's still wearing his bike
helmet, and when he takes it off, I want to smooth his hair.
We embark on a staring contest. He pulls out his earbuds
and holds them in his hand and steps closer. I've memorized
him, every inch of visible skin, but I haven't met his eyes
for this long since camp. I'd forgotten how dark they are.
Undoubtedly the most beautiful eyes I've ever seen. Huge,
chocolate brown, and heavily lashed. Tatya Nadine tells me

to avoid boys with "bedroom eyes." *"Gorestnoe sobytie."* Heartbreakers, she warns. I never understood what she meant until Josh.

He opens his mouth, but before he can say anything, Emma flies through the door. She takes one look at me and senses bad news. In a flash, she's standing between me and Josh, who slips the buds back into his ears and walks away. He knows Emma and Isaac barely tolerate him.

"What did you hear?" she asks.

It's easier to say it the second time, and I repeat what I told Megan. My heart beats so strong that I can feel my pulse in my wrists and neck, like my body is reminding me that I need to keep moving, keep breathing.

We're supposed to spread out, one student per table as we review the papers. Instead of sitting in her usual spot, Emma plops into the chair next to mine. Isaac barely beats the bell. Megan gives him enough time to fill his mug, and then she directs everyone to huddle around me.

"You too, Josh."

He sits in the next room, a closet really, that houses two Macs equipped with the software to design the paper and maintain the website. A gift from some alum who got rich in Silicon Valley. Josh is accustomed to ignoring us; he doesn't even turn around. Megan crosses the room and gently pulls out an earbud. "Come," she says. "Today, you're editorial."

Josh's floppy hair covers his face. When he brushes it back, he looks confused and disgruntled, but when his eyes meet mine again, he loses his annoyed expression and smiles. He takes a seat at the adjoining table, right behind me. He gently nudges my foot with his.

Megan speaks on my behalf, passing around the papers and explaining Ivan the Photographer and my officially missing father. Ukraine dominates the front pages of each newspaper. A photo of a barn on fire. A cow, dead, lying next to the flames. People clustered a safe distance away from the burning building. Ukraine, Ukraine, Ukraine—the word popping off the page.

"This is your assignment. Read the earthquake stories. Isaac, I want you to research the photographer and put together his publication history. Emma, do an image search and let's see if we can get an idea of what this area looks like. Map it if you can. Charlotte, take a look at CNN world news and the BBC. Maybe try Ukrainian news sites and see what they're reporting locally."

"I speak Russian, not Ukrainian. They're close, but not the same language—you know, like Mandarin and Cantonese. I don't know the Cyrillic alphabet."

Emma elbows me. "Then check out TV and radio sites. You won't have to read that way."

"Good call," Megan says. "Josh, you're with me. We'll look

40

at the Red Cross and Doctors Without Borders to get a sense of the damage."

I'm grateful that she doesn't use the word "casualties."

We retreat to our usual seats. I'm not sure if this is a real assignment or Megan's act of kindness, a distraction, something to keep me busy, something to make me feel not so helpless.

It almost works.

Six

We search and compare notes:

Cell towers down.

Power out.

Emergency services overwhelmed.

Roads blocked and damaged.

Aid groups compiling lists of the missing.

Families beginning to be reunited.

Ivan the Photographer is accomplished and respected.

Not a thing about Dad or the French dude, Pascal. I spend the morning with my friends, searching so silently that I can hear their breathing and Emma's growling stomach. Dad is missing, but I'm not alone.

Every five minutes, Emma asks me how I'm doing. Isaac refills my coffee cup like a diner waitress. Megan and Josh offer sympathetic smiles.

My eyes are on him as much as the computer screen.

As we pack up at the end of class, Josh takes the seat next to me. "I don't have your number," he says.

"I don't have yours, either."

He produces a Sharpie and writes his number on the back of my hand. I'm counting the galaxy of freckles covering his arm, searching for Orion and the Big and Little Dippers. Those freckles.

I sleepwalk through the rest of the day. It's like I borrowed Harry Potter's invisibility cloak and no one can see me in the sea of the other three thousand kids who go to my school. Teachers don't greet me. No one calls on me. I've never been so grateful to be ignored, so ready for the weekend.

My only comfort is tracing Josh's number on my skin, the thick black ink.

When the final bell rings, we cluster at our lockers. Emma convinces Isaac that his priority is helping her with chem. "Come with us," she says.

Isaac follows us to the Blue Danube Café, which has decent after-school snacks and plenty of open tables. We claim the back corner.

"Watch out," Em says. "There's a bee."

Isaac yanks off his sneaker and squashes the bug right on the table.

"Super hygienic," I say. "But smooth."

Isaac is gentlemanly and old-fashioned. He's coppery from head to toe, with dark curly hair, even curlier than mine, amber-colored eyes, and almost the same shade of skin. Until this year, he wore a tie to school. Every day. Even with T-shirts. He's unusual in all the right ways.

We move to a large table closer to the window. When Emma returns from the counter, she places a pot of tea between us. "You okay?" she asks.

"Yeah. Just stressed," I say. "Tea will help. Thanks."

I read and reread the same three pages of *Beloved* before putting the book down. I have nine chapters to go, and I have to finish it this weekend. Em and Isaac make progress on her chemistry assignment. She writes her notes so hard and fast that I can't believe she doesn't perforate the pages.

I take out my camera and flip through shots from last Sunday, pictures of Mom and Dad at the farmers market. In one picture, Mom holds a bouquet of flowers, orange Chinese lanterns and starbursts of white and yellow dahlias. A blooming constellation that makes her look magical. Dad points to something in the bay, and Mom's eyes follow his.

She looks so much stronger when she's with him, but as soon as he goes on a trip, she transforms, becoming almost fragile, a cracking glass figurine. I compare the photo to my memory of last night, when we sat with Uncle Miguel. Her raccoon eye makeup and silence.

Dad's her anchor. He keeps her feet on the ground. I swear she'll float into the clouds if he doesn't come home. I'll lose them both. Orphaned.

I turn off my camera and pick up my book and sip my cooling tea. Emma's phone buzzes with a text. She puts her pencil down, and I catch it as it rolls off the table.

"Party tomorrow night," she says. "Remember that guy Nicholas who graduated a few years ago? He's hosting in his new apartment. It's mandatory. You MUST go. No matter what. Promise now. Blood oath. I insist."

Isaac mimes slashing open his palm and shakes Em's hand. They turn to me, waiting, knowing I'm waffling, knowing that parties kind of make me nervous. I flirt with social anxiety; I'm not a serious case, just enough to be intimidated by large groups of people, especially if there's dancing. I was born a wallflower.

"Maybe," I say. "I'll have to check with my mom. I need to work in the bakery in the morning." And I have to go for a run. Anything to get out all of this nervous energy.

"Unacceptable," Emma says.

Isaac nods. "Yep. And you have to leave that"—he points to my camera—"at home. You look like a stalker when you bring it to parties. Or paparazzi. Not good."

They are relentless and giddy and won't take no for an answer. They are contagious.

"Okay, but you know, with my dad—"

Emma cuts me off. "We know, Charlotte. Of course. If anything happens, we'll come to your house for a sleepover. But there's no way in hell we're leaving you alone all weekend. You'd need to get a restraining order." She looks at her naked wrist, pretending to check a watch. "It's after five. Too late to see a judge. You're stuck with us."

This is what it must feel like to have siblings who boss you around and love you because you belong together. Bound by blood and home and so many other tangible and intangible things.

I wasn't supposed to be an only child, and I don't know how, but I miss the sister I never met. A fundamental longing that's always with me. Lena died when she was a baby, just a year before I was born. Sudden infant death syndrome. Mom put her down for a nap, and Lena never woke up. I've always looked at friends with brothers and sisters with such envy. I want to share a room and share parents, share clothes and vacations. I want someone else at home when Dad's gone and Mom's in the bakery. I'd welcome rivalry and arguments if it meant that I didn't have to live in such a quiet house.

Emma and I met the first day of sixth grade. She was reading manga, a book based on a show that I'd watched for the last month straight, staying up until two in the morning without my parents knowing. Emma and I were in love with the same character. I remember not wanting to share Emma with anyone else. If I could have sold an organ or all of my furniture to have her as family, I would have. Would still. Because I can't imagine anyone being more of a sister to me than her. We've applied to the same colleges so we can be roommates. I wish we were conjoined twins.

I pretend to stab my finger and raise it in the air. "Okay. I swear I'll spend the weekend with you."

"Thank God that's settled," Em says. "Now we need to finish chem BECAUSE IT'S KILLING ME."

An old man at the counter turns and glares at us. My signal to leave.

"Enough with the yelling," I say. "Don't get us kicked out of our favorite café." I hug them both good-bye, understanding how Dad makes Mom feel: rooted and safe. I can't imagine going through this without Emma and Isaac.

When I get home, the door is gaping open. I inch forward and peek inside, scared. My heart beats harder when I remember that Mom isn't supposed to be back for another hour or two, depending on bridge traffic. All of the wholesale places she and Nadine go to are in the East Bay.

We always lock the door. Mom and Dad drilled this into me as much as they taught me to look both ways when crossing the street. We live on Clement Street in the Richmond District, which used to be unknown to tourists unless they were lost finding their way to the Golden Gate Bridge. Not anymore. A few restaurants opened. A couple of cafés. Some shops, including Green Apple, my favorite bookstore. Now everyone wants to live in one of the two-story stucco buildings painted the same pastel hues as Easter candy. Now the sidewalks are crowded and we have to pay more attention to our surroundings. In San Francisco, the more popular the neighborhood, the more break-ins.

Then I smell Dad's lasagna, and I convince myself that this was all a ruse. He decided to come right back home. We couldn't reach him because he left his phone in airplane mode. He's going to jump out and surprise me and say he discovered a punk polka band.

I almost smile.

Then I see Mom.

"I thought you were going shopping," I say. I try not to sound disappointed because I'm happy to see her, even if it's a surprise, even if I wish it were Dad instead.

I follow her into the kitchen. She's made a salad and baked two different kinds of cookies.

"Nadine went without me. I should be with you," she says.

"You haven't heard anything?" I ask.

She shakes her head. "I'll tell you when I do. *Obeshchaniye.*" Promise. "Did he forget something and have to come back to get it?" she asks.

I'm accustomed to not picking up after Dad when he's traveling—which, according to superstition, only invites disaster. His sweatshirt drapes over one of the kitchen chairs and will remain until he walks through the door. It's bad luck to return to the house if you forgot something.

I shake my head. "No, Mom. He didn't." I want to reassure her that he didn't break a mirror, sit on a table, or whistle in the house, either—actions that bring misfortune. "Everything was normal."

She nods. "Okay."

She sifts powdered sugar over a tray of Russian wedding cookies, my favorite when I was little. When she wipes hair from her face, she leaves a comet streak of sugar across her forehead. I gesture to her. "You got some on you."

"Let me change," she says. "Go ahead and serve the lasagna. I thought we could watch a movie while we eat."

She's cleared off the coffee table to make room for dinner. The TV is on, the news muted, jumping to the next big story. A train derailed somewhere in New Jersey. I wonder how long it will take them to forget about the quake, if Dad will be home before Ukraine fades entirely from the news.

Mom emerges in yoga pants and one of Dad's T-shirts, almost dress-length. It makes her look younger and a little lost. We're used to his trips, to his prepared meals tiding us over until he's home, but this is different. We both feel it—I

49

can tell. We're in limbo. I pull out my phone, but the only texts I have are from Emma and Isaac about the torture that is chemistry. I toss it onto the table.

Mom picks up the remote. "That sci-fi movie is on, the one you wanted to see in the theater. Want to watch it?"

"Yeah," I say. "That's great." A perfect escape. Aliens and intergalactic warfare.

Mom's a multitasker. When we all watch movies together, she usually has a project, paying bills or making grocery lists or looking at new recipes to attract non-Russians to the bakery. She can't sit still, especially if she's sitting next to me. Not tonight, though. She doesn't busy herself with something else.

Last summer, I had a crush on one of the actors in this film, but that wore off. The plot doesn't absorb me like I hoped it would. I want to be swept away by action and hotness. Instead, I stifle a yawn. I know I won't sleep. Not a chance, especially since I haven't gone for a run since before Dad left. I'll stay awake all night picturing him who knows where. I'll count stars and wish him home.

I try to quash my worry that this evening with Mom will be fleeting, a spell due to expire at midnight. As we watch the movie, I fake tiredness and rest my head on her shoulder, thrilled when she squeezes my hand and doesn't let go. We sit for much longer than I expect. When the moment finally comes to an end, she murmurs an apology as she fetches the cookies from the kitchen.

When she returns, she positions herself against the arm of the couch—not where she was before, not near me. I don't accept her usual distance, not now. I scoot over and put my head in her lap. She pats my back, quick and light. I take what I can get.

"Vsyo budet v poryadke," she says. Everything will be okay. "He'll be home soon."

I wonder if this is the price: The only way I get her affection is if Dad is gone. Not just working, but missing.

Seven

I wake with a jolt. It's still dark, but when I see that it's five o'clock in the morning, I know that Mom's already downstairs. She's not a natural morning person, but bakers rise before dawn in order to offer fresh, warm pastries to the world. Plus, I doubt she slept at all.

Photos cover my walls, some framed, others tacked or taped. A giant collage. Mom and Dad and Emma and Isaac. A couple of covert ones of Josh. Snapshots and my attempt at more formal portraits. Some darkroom failures. When Dad comes home, I'll take a picture of him every day. Mom, too, and Nadine, and my friends. I'll shoot each person I love. I'll immortalize—not memorialize. I'll make sure I *see* them, appreciate them, and not take them for granted.

When I open the door to the store, I'm filled with the same warmth I feel every time I work in the bakery. Tatya Nadine prepares the cases and counter as Mom preheats the last of the steel-gray ovens. I'm relieved to see Tatya even though it's her day off. I need her, but Mom needs her even more.

Everything about Tatya Nadine is soft: her round body and velveteen tracksuit and poufy hair, dyed magenta, the same shade she paints her nails. Her swollen toes peek out from her shimmery gold sandals. She's taller than Mom, taller than me, and it's a relief to be embraced by someone substantial. When I hug Mom, I'm self-conscious because of my height, only five six, but four inches taller than her. I feel like a giraffe hugging a baby bunny.

Nadine hands me a mug of coffee and asks, "Doing okay?"

"Yeah. Just worried."

"I'm here," she says. "And remember to take care of your mama. She needs you now."

"I will, Tatya. Promise." I brush a cloud of flour from her sleeve, and she gives me another hug.

Past the long row of cases, past the cash register, is the butter-yellow kitchen. It's small, with one wall of ovens, another of baking racks, and several metal counters and wooden butcher blocks. I pull my apron off its hook.

Mom smiles. She and I match in our well-worn aprons. As always, the kitchen fills with quiet concentration. There's barely room for two bodies, a constant negotiation of space.

Mom nods her head to the side when she wants to slip by, a precise movement more efficient than words. I tap her shoulder instead of muttering, *Excuse me.* You can hear us slap dough, chop fruit, and open cans, but you rarely hear our voices. We communicate through food and with our bodies, by pointing to a pan, by passing flour, sugar, and butter.

We begin with the delicate pastries first, the thin layered dough, before moving on to the savory. We fill the shelves with loaves of bread, mainly light and dark rye. My favorite is *kalach,* a round loaf that looks like a dish with two handles. By seven o'clock, the glass cases teem with ornate layer cakes and a pastel rainbow of meringues. We cater to Russians, Ukrainians, and Poles, but we make sure we have wider appeal. Last year, I trained Nadine on the new espresso machine, and she serves a decent latte to the college students up the hill. Mom makes the best apple turnovers in San Francisco, or so states the faded "Cheap Eats" review posted in the front window, which praises her flaky crust and gleaming sugar crystals.

Mom and I labor over the crown jewel of Russian cakes: Bird's Milk, *Ptichye Moloko,* a white crème soufflé cake covered with chocolate. We have a saying, "You have everything but Bird's Milk." Meaning, if you have everything but the cake, you have it all. Eartha Kitt has a song that talks about feeding her lover Bird's Milk. Dad sings it whenever he eats a slice. As I bake alongside Mom, safe and warm in the confines of the kitchen, tears fill my eyes. If Dad were here, all of us together, the saying would be true for me.

The cake requires intense concentration. Once the soufflé sets and the cake has cooled, I watch Mom coat it with a thick layer of chocolate ganache, not a fingerprint or smudge anywhere. My hands tremble as I add a flourish of roses in pink icing. The cake serves thirty, and we'll sell out by the end of the day, each slice so otherworldly, so perfect.

"You've gotten good at decorating," Mom says. "You can always work here more. I bet you could be as good as me in no time."

I look at Mom and then the cake. Mom's first language is Russian, then food, and third is English. I feel like she's inviting me into her world. I'd be tempted to quit cross-country if she really wants me here more. I'd exchange running for her in a heartbeat.

"Maybe," I say, worried she'll take it back or forget or never invite me again.

The door creaks open, and in her smoker's voice, Nadine welcomes a customer. It's Boris, a man who resembles an emaciated goldfish, complete with bulging googly eyes. He owns the watch repair shop across the street and always comes about this time for piroshki. They talk about the neighborhood, whether or not they will add more buses to the crowded 38 line, and they muse about the fog. They've had the same conversation for years. Boris pays and Tatya Nadine chimes, *"Prijatnogo appétit."* Bon appétit.

After two hours, Mom withdraws her last pan from the oven, an apricot strudel. We tidy up after our morning's work in order to prepare for the next day. Nadine is scared of heights, so I join her behind the counter and climb up the ladder to change the sign with wobbly chalk, listing tomorrow's specials.

Mom and Tatya Nadine free me after the morning rush. I return to our apartment upstairs and change into running shorts. I have time for a long run down the beach and back— usually my favorite way to spend a Saturday afternoon. Running and taking pictures. After grabbing my camera and stretching, I go downstairs to pick up the bank deposit. When Nadine hands it to me, it feels heavy, the satisfying result of a busy morning. She wraps her arms around me, holding tight. "Try not to worry too much," she says. "He'll come home soon."

Mom emerges from the kitchen and takes my hand. "She's right, Charlotte. It's going to be okay. *Poka.*" Bye for now.

When I glance back at the store, Mom and Tatya Nadine are standing at the counter, looking more like mother and daughter than ever. They'll spend the rest of the afternoon in the bakery, quietly reading the newspaper, pausing to nibble from the day-old basket. When I was little, I would snuggle between them, not caring that their attention was on the news. Tatya Nadine would stroke my hair and I would lean closer to Mom, yearning for her to do the same, happy when I felt her fingers brush my scalp. Gestures can be more important than words.

I inhale the smell of steamed dumplings and nearly collide with Bobby Zhou, our neighbor who graduated from my school last year. We ran cross-country together. "Watch it, Charlotte." A giant take-out order fills his arms. "I've got to get this to the senior center."

I don't want to be rude, so I say, "I'll walk with you. Need help?"

"I got it."

I eye Bobby, who has an aspiring Goth style including a long black trench coat and asymmetrical hair that drapes over his left eye. Ever the rebel, Bobby quit working at his family's restaurant and accepted a position at the Sanrio store across the street. To meet girls, he insisted. There, he sat behind the register in the center of an impressive Hello Kitty spiral. Oversized plush Hello Kitty dolls next to winking Hello Kitty backpacks, and a multitude of Hello Kitty school supplies. Bobby guarded the key to the pricey things displayed in the glass case—alarm clocks and watches and pendants. He was unaware of how his delicate features blended in with the sweet figurines, how his pout only made him more appropriate for the job.

I wanted to take his picture and make him a sign: LOOK AT ME: I'M THE PORTRAIT OF IRONY.

Last month, he made manager and then abruptly quit. No one knows why he returned to pushing dim sum carts.

"Later," he says.

"Bye. And, Bobby?"

"What?"

"You may want to change your clothes before you go back. You reek of pot."

He looks startled. "I thought the kitchen covered up the smell."

"Not unless you're making weed dumplings."

"Crap," Bobby says. "Thanks."

I jog down Clement Street, dodging shoppers browsing the Chinese markets' produce stands. When I reach Golden Gate Park, I start to run in earnest, cruising up to the luminescent Conservatory of Flowers, slowing down to admire the Victorian structure and its delicate glass panes. I struggle to leave the treasured view behind as I continue up the path.

I travel past the congested areas of the park and into the meadows. This is my favorite part of the city, the long stretch of green ending at the ocean. I let the breeze carry me, racing the seagulls. I pass Stow Lake, with its rented paddleboats, and Strawberry Hill, the island of my lost virginity. His name is Kyle. He was a mistake. I reach Chain of Lakes, and I don't pause until I'm near the end of the park, at the Dutch Windmill and Queen Wilhelmina Tulip Garden.

This is Dad's favorite spot in the park, especially when the feathery parrot tulips are in full bloom, just a few weeks from now. We walk here often, standing beneath the windmill, giant and hovering at the very end of the garden. I don't know how to occupy a city of memories: his favorite views and restaurants and bookstores. It's one thing to navigate the apartment and see his things. It's another to venture into the world and still have everything remind me of him.

It hits me again, the full force of our situation. That he's missing. That I don't know when we'll see him again. All I want is to walk through the front door and find him stretched out in his favorite chair, exhausted from his trip and happy to be home. When will that happen? *Will* it happen? I feel pain in my side, but it's not a stitch from running. It's panic, and the only way I know how to deal with it is to run harder.

I sprint directly into the wind and endure the sand in my face. The highway curves and disappears into Lands End, the most accurately named place in the world. I gaze at the Golden Gate Bridge below and the soft hills in the distance. I turn to look out at the ocean, a wide expanse of shimmering blue, and remember Megan's words. *Stay positive. No news is good news.* I try to outrun worry. Outrun fear.

When I reach the water, I face the Pacific and feel the waves spray my face. My skin and clothes absorb the salt water, and the sensation is an unexpected relief. We Russians have stories about water spirits that bless those who wade into pure and sacred water, so powerful that it protects from evil spirits, heals the sick, and resurrects the dead. I need to remember Dad's strength, his height and sense of humor and the crafty way he can get anyone to talk.

My mind fills with a mantra, a plea: *Vozvrashchat'sya. Vozvrashchat'sya. Vozvrashchat'sya.* Come back.

Eight

We stand before a three-story Victorian in the Mission District, a hipster neighborhood where bookstores and cafés nestle between taquerias and Mexican grocers. Music blares through the open windows upstairs. Silhouettes of people fill a rounded room that reminds me of a castle turret. This is my most difficult moment, right before I walk into a party.

"Come on," Emma says. "You'll be fine after a beer." We climb the stairs. A step wobbles under my weight. The sign taped to the front door instructs us to go to the third floor.

To my relief, we find Isaac in the kitchen. "About time," he says. "Get a beverage from the cooler."

I reach into the melting ice and grab a beer for Em and a Sprite for me. The last thing I want is to feel foggy or cotton-headed. My heart feels a little shaky, and I don't want to risk bursting into tears in the middle of a party. They say alcohol is an acquired taste, and I have yet to develop a desire for it. Maybe in college. Maybe never.

"Hand it over." Isaac takes Emma's bottle, wedges it under a kitchen drawer handle, and snaps off the cap. "I love multi-purpose cabinetry."

I look around the room full of strangers. I don't recognize anyone, a relief. Tonight, I prefer anonymity.

Everyone seems older, graduates, free from high school. They're tattooed and pierced and liberated. I look down at my skirt and wonder if they can tell that I'm not one of them. Highly likely.

Em blends in. Isaac can talk to anybody, make anybody laugh and spill their secrets. He's more like Dad than me that way. A natural.

I miss my camera.

I don't know if Josh was already here or just arrived. He stands there looking at me. I feel that pull again, like my feet will walk over before my brain commands them to move. He nods to the door, one I hadn't noticed. When he pulls it open, I tell Em and Isaac that I'll be back and leave before they have the opportunity to give me hell about my taste in boys.

The back steps feel as substantial as kindling. I don't dare lean against the railing, but I need something to prop me up.

Josh sits on the top stair, which miraculously remains

intact. He's wearing this army-green jacket that I love. It's buttoned all the way up with these small pewter buttons embossed with a design I can't make out. I've never been close enough. I want to feel each one, work them through the fabric. I should return to the kitchen before I make a fool of myself. I'm not convinced I can keep my hands to myself.

"I've been thinking about you," he says. "About your dad. Any news?"

I take a seat and a long sip of soda—a gulp, really. The stairs are smaller than I thought, and I wind up closer to him than I intend. He doesn't move away. He actually inches closer.

It's an eagle, in silhouette, on his buttons.

"I'm trying not to think about it. Megan told me to stay positive, but it's hard when I'm terrified that he's never going to come home."

"Okay," he says, smiling and picking at the label on his beer, peeling back the corner. I want him to do the same to my shirt. "How's that working out for you?"

"Miserable failure."

From this high up, I can see most of the block, yards filled with paper lanterns, container gardens, and clotheslines. Lights twinkle from the base of Bernal Hill. This part of the city feels so charged, so full of life. Bolder colors and personalities than in my quiet, foggy neighborhood.

Josh nudges me with his elbow. He stares at his hands, not at me. "You know, I didn't expect to see you here tonight. I don't think of you as the partying type. I'm glad you came."

"What type am I?" I'm able to look at him for longer than five seconds without feeling faint. A miracle.

"I haven't figured that out yet," he says right before draining his beer and wiping his mouth on his sleeve. Who knew one could envy clothing.

We've been in the same English class for three years. He's always been a distraction, cute and outspoken and daring—not dangerous like Emma and Isaac think. But it wasn't until he joined the paper last year that he occupied more and more space in my head. He signed a lease and now resides there permanently.

Then multimedia camp at Berkeley. For the first time, we sat together at meals, groggy in the morning and totally awake at dinner. We talked nonstop. I couldn't help myself with him. He lifted the spell that cursed my house with silence. He coaxed me out, patient and listening—*really* listening. When my sentences trailed off, he stopped and asked me to complete my thoughts. He was curious and paid attention and has those eyes and lips, full, and all I wanted to do was touch them with my finger and then my mouth.

And I did.

Now he meets my eyes and kisses me again. I don't dare unbutton his jacket, but I run my fingertip over the pewter, tracing the eagle's wings. Something about being with him, touching, makes me less self-conscious, like all I care about is skin touching skin. Maybe it's how he reaches for me, how he puts his hand on the back of my head, his fingers in my hair. The surety of it.

He pulls away, and I feel so happy—beyond belief crazy happy—but there's something else in the pit of my stomach, something I hate to admit. Having him want me makes me remember all of the times in my life that I feel unwanted. Like I'm never enough. I can't let him see this, how suddenly everything feels bittersweet, so I kiss him again. I wish I could say it's because I'm bold and confident instead of hiding my real feelings.

He laughs when my lips meet his, like we have an inside joke.

When he pulls away he says, "I was going to ask if you'd see a movie with me tonight, but I'm stuck here. I'm not at this party by choice. This is my brother's place, and I stay over when my dad is away for work and my mom has an overnight shift. Nurse. Overprotective. But you should know that I wanted to hang out."

I push it down—the insecurity and the fear—so it's rumbling in my stomach and not tangling my head and heart.

"We should do that sometime," I say casually, as though I'm not such a whirling dervish of emotion. "Do you like staying with your brother?"

"Yeah," he says. "I'm going to move in here after graduation. There's a big age difference between us. Eleven years. Technically, he's my half brother. He left for college when I was six. We're really close now, though." He pauses a second. "Hey, with everything that's going on with your dad . . . We talked about everything at camp, and I know you have your friends, but I thought . . . maybe . . . you can always talk to me. Or come over. You can just come over and *not* talk too."

"Thanks," I say. "Really."

We sit and look at each other, not knowing what else to say. He reaches for my hand and traces my palm, the inside of each finger, and my body feels entirely new, like a piece of clothing I just bought and am wearing for the first time. I worry I'm breathing too hard. When he kisses me again, I inhale every part of him, every molecule. This time, I don't have to pretend to be bold.

I inch closer. My palm remains in his hand.

He touches my hair, and I can't control my breathing. "I once tried to count your curls. I sat behind you last year, in English, and every time you moved your head, I had to start over. I think you have an infinite number of curls."

"They drive me crazy."

"I love them," he says.

"You've liked me for that long? Since last year?"

"I've liked you for as long as you've liked me," he says, smiling.

"It was that obvious?" I ask.

"Yeah, when I joined the paper."

I shake my head and smile to myself. Dad taught me to play poker in first grade. I'm the best bluffer in the house. "Sophomore-year English. I liked you for a year before you joined the paper."

When he says he's liked me even longer than that, I can't tell if he's joking. I guess it doesn't matter. Not now.

"Want a tour of this place? My brother Ian's a photographer. I don't think I ever told you that."

"No," I say. "You didn't. And he lives with that guy Nicholas?"

"Yeah, worlds colliding. Come on. I need another beer. How about you?" He reaches for my Sprite. "No beer?"

"I don't like how it tastes," I say.

I can barely squeeze through the kitchen door. The party doubled in size while I was with Josh. I spot about five other seniors mingling in the packed kitchen, only acquaintances. As I struggle through the crowd, someone grabs my hand and pulls me into the next room.

"There you are," Emma says. "I've been waiting for you to come back." She sees Josh. "Hi."

It's not that Emma's unfriendly exactly. She's *cordial.* Josh picks up on it and raises a hand like he's waving hello from across the street or something.

"Come on, Charlotte," he says. "I want to show you something."

Then Emma mouths, *Go.* She knows how much I've wanted this, his attention, especially with what's going on with Dad. She doesn't like him, but she understands how he makes me feel.

I follow Josh down the hall into the living room, the room I saw from outside. Everyone's in the kitchen and dining room now, where the food is. We have the living room to ourselves. The color blows me away.

"Ian calls this aquamarine," Josh says. "He wants it to look like the beach. He's making a table out of driftwood."

Even though I grew up blocks from the ocean, I've never seen water this color. A tropical, clear blue. Between the shape and shade of the room, I feel like I'm swimming.

Even the old worn couch, low to the ground like a raft on waves, fits in. Black-and-white framed photos cover a part of the wall from floor to ceiling. I walk over to get a better look. They're landscapes of various beaches, each labeled in gallery signage, spots of the coast starting in Baja and moving north to Washington State. Waves crash in one, and another captures a long stretch of sand. They're haunting in their stillness, but the settings are so distinct.

"He's been to all of these places?" I ask.

Josh nods. "Me too. We went on a road trip last summer. It was incredible. I filmed each beach and then compiled the clips so it looks like one day of low and high tide, but on different beaches. They blend into one another."

"You really like making films," I say, not a question.

"It's all I want to do. We'll see if I get in anywhere, given my many behavior problems and disciplinary actions." He rolls his eyes. "Good SAT scores can't balance out suspensions. That's what Principal Levi says, anyway." He smiles, but bashfully.

I can't think about college, not now with Dad missing. Too much stress. I return my eyes to the beach photos and ask Josh if he has a favorite.

He doesn't pause and walks straight to a shot of a crescent-shaped beach surrounded by towering trees where the forest meets the water. "This one. Hug Point, Oregon. Have you been?"

I shake my head.

"Put it on your list. At low tide, there are caves filled with shells, and the rocks are round."

"Round?"

Josh heads to a set of bookshelves and returns with a clear bowl filled with what looks like small cannonballs. "Pick one up."

It's heavy, and as I cradle it in my palm, I notice the small holes and ridges. Anywhere else, the rock would have been flat and smooth.

"How?" I ask.

"Part of the shore is a slab of rock, so when they roll back and forth, some become perfectly round," he says. "I became kind of obsessed with them. I brought back a lot. *A lot.* It amazes me that a rock can go from flat to round. That something can change its shape like that. It made me think of all the things that can evolve, you know? I guess it just takes a ton of patience. I tell myself that, anyway."

"I'm not that patient," I say, thinking of Dad. I clutch the rock hard, squeezing it as I think of all the pictures of crumbled buildings and the injured. The images and anxiety come hard and fast, almost like an assault. Beads of sweat collect along my hairline. My head balloons, and I suddenly feel a little light-headed.

"Are you okay?" Josh asks.

"Yeah." I nod, trying to discreetly take a deep breath. It was a mistake coming here, being with all of these people. Even if Mom ends up hiding in her room all night, I should be home with her.

"Really?"

"I'm just tired. I think it's time for me to go home. You know, with everything that's going on." I roll the stone between my hands one last time before holding it out, palm outstretched. "Here."

He steps closer and covers my hand with his own. "You keep it," he says.

He steadies me, and all of a sudden, I want him, not just his touch, not just another kiss, but *him*. Searching for him in the cafeteria and secretly staring at him in class will no longer do. I want him next to me all day, every day.

"Thanks." I clutch the rock, now warm from my skin. I take another deep breath and look him in the eye. "Did you mean it?" I ask.

"Yes, keep it. Really," he says. He squeezes my hand, pressing the rock deeper into my palm.

"No." I shake my head. "Did you mean what you said? That you've liked me all this time?"

"Yes. I meant it." He squeezes my hand one more time before leaning in. His kiss feels like mouth-to-mouth resuscitation, and my breathing slows. So does my heartbeat. By the time he pulls away, I'm almost steady.

It feels right to be with him. Especially now. I grip the rock. He's given me more than the rock to hold on to.

Nine

Thanks to the Renaissance fair in Golden Gate Park, cus-
tomers in medieval velvet gowns and black cloaks flood the
bakery early Sunday morning. A long line snakes out the
door and down the busy street. At one point, Bobby pops in
to inspect the commotion, fearing a holdup or some other
sensational explanation for the sudden craving for Russian
baked goods. Only once before, thanks to a spontaneous
engagement party, have we ever sold out the store. Mom
woke me early, asked if I'd help out. Turns out I slept with
the rock, clinging to it like a teddy bear.

I'm tired from the party, but that doesn't last long. I race
from counter to kitchen as we pop tray after tray of cookies and pastries into the oven. Steam clouds the glass cases.
We stay open for an extra three hours, and the time flies
by. I counted up two weeks' worth of profits after one busy
day, the equivalent of finding a large bundle of bills on the

sidewalk. Happy with such easy success, Nadine and Mom insist we celebrate.

During the day, Mom said just a few sentences to me, mostly directions, with a final "Job well done." Now, she laughs at Tatya Nadine's jokes. At first, her laugh sounds unfamiliar, but after a while, I remember this is how she can be. She's the same when the sun comes out after weeks of fog, so low and thick that it feels like you're choking on clouds.

The wine helps. Dad keeps the fridge stocked with beer, and we always have wine for Mom and something for Tatya Nadine, who picks a bottle of Prosecco and liberates the cork with a smile.

We chop mounds of onions and cabbage. Russian pastries are complicated, but our savory food is comforting. Mom kneads dough for the vegetable pie as Tatya Nadine seasons the soup, tasting it after adding each herb.

"Charlotte," Mom says, her voice sounding lighter than it has since Dad left. Since he disappeared. "Why don't you change? And please set the table."

My shirt looks like an edible Jackson Pollock painting. My room's a mess, and I've hauled more boxes of photos from my closet. So much for my outstanding organizational skills. Snapshots of Dad are scattered on the floor. I reach down and tidy them into little piles, promising myself that I'll clean up later.

I'm out of clean clothes. Only skirts and dresses hang in my closet. Summer clothes. I choose the most casual but feel silly and overdressed. It's fine, though—appropriate for a celebration.

Tatya Nadine smiles when she sees me. *"Vy posmotrite dovol'no."* You look pretty. She hands me a glass of Prosecco. I shake my head. "Mom will freak out."

"Are you saying you only drink on Christmas? You've never had a drink at a party?" She laughs as she dares me to answer.

"Okay then, yes please."

When Mom reenters the kitchen, I almost drop the glass, worried her disapproval might ruin her mood. She's changed too, into a rose-colored shirt and jeans. It's as though she stepped out of my favorite photo in the hallway, the one framed in hand-carved wood and layered in gold leaf. In the picture, my parents stand in front of the War Memorial Opera House, my young father dashing in a tuxedo and my mother in a dress the exact same color as the shirt she's wearing now. Her rose garden gown. Beaded flowers climb the length of the dress, circling the waist and blooming at the shoulders. Just as she had twenty years earlier, she's twisted her hair into a bun, revealing her long neck.

She looks younger, but more than that, she looks content. So much so that it takes me a moment to notice the left side of her face, the subtle droop, a permanent reminder of her stroke and my violent entrance into the world. While uneven, both of her eyes look almost cheery. Her forehead has lost its tight worry lines; her jaw is relaxed; and her mouth— finally—curves into a genuine smile.

Tatya raises her glass. *"Za vashe zdaroveeye ee blag-apaloocheeye."* To health and happiness. Mom clinks hers against Nadine's.

Mom surveys the food steaming on the table. "This reminds me of being back home."

Tatya Nadine nods. "This is my babushka's soup."

"I could never cook as well as my grandmother," Mom says. "You know how many times I've tried. I'm glad Jeremiah had the chance to eat her food before she passed away. She liked him. He was the first boyfriend of mine she liked. Even though he's American. I still can't believe that."

Mom's family wasn't political, but a few worked in government, low-ranking officials. Her cousin in the agriculture department was the first one to reach any kind of stature. Mom describes him as a cunning politician.

Mom turns to me. "My grandmother would have changed her opinion if she'd seen your father at the White Nights Festival."

When Mom talks about growing up in Russia, she doesn't sound wistful. She lists the people and landmarks she misses most, but she talks about how life is so much easier here. She describes how she loves Russian summers but dreads how the snow and ice drain the world of all its color. Besides her family, what she misses the most are the White Nights, when, from May until July, twilight lasts until dawn. The White Nights embody an in-between time, with the sky barely light, yet streetlamps illuminate the riverfront. Given our current state of waiting, I have a new appreciation for the prolonged dusk. Think of a sunset that lasts for hours, how the brilliant colors slowly fade into a pink pastel light. I wonder how long the sun and moon occupy the same sky, and in that moment, I want nothing more than to take photos of Mom's homeland, a family vacation, the three of us. Maybe Tatya could come too.

As Mom passes the bread basket to Nadine, she talks about how Dad came back to St. Petersburg to do an anniversary piece a year after the Neva River flooded. Really an excuse to see Mom again. They'd kept in touch through airmail and late-night phone calls. He came for the White Nights Festival. I've read his article about the trip, how a rainbow of clouds streaked across the sky creating an exquisite backdrop for the czar's Winter Palace.

"He splurged for a boat ride. He couldn't afford it, and the paper didn't cover that kind of expense. Your dad can be extravagant, Charlotte. Back then, he'd spend all his money on his phone bill and beer and music. Without me, he probably still would.

"We went up the river to see the islands. I wanted to show him the burial place of the czars and their families. Our driver met another motorboat, and he decided to race. He'd been drinking. We didn't know it, though, and the other boat certainly didn't know what was going on. What a surprise."

She laughs, and it takes everything I have to stay in my seat and not get up and hug her.

"Our boat almost collided with theirs," she says. "They were classical musicians, and they'd been driving very slowly to protect their instruments. One man waved his violin in the air and screamed at us."

"Words we won't repeat now," Tatya Nadine says, raising an eyebrow at Mom, who doesn't feel the same need to shelter me from the profanity I use liberally.

Mom cocks an eyebrow in return, laughing. She takes another sip of wine. "Fine." This is why they resemble mother and daughter more than sisters: Nadine's bossiness and Mom's almost petulant responses.

"This was before the fireworks started and more boats cruised past us," Mom says. "Our driver didn't care about them. He just wanted to beat the musicians. They were shouting, and one of them threw a music stand at our boat. He hit the driver smack on the forehead." She strokes a spot above her brow. "He wasn't too hurt, but he couldn't see through the blood gushing down his face. Your father didn't know how to drive the boat. I hiked up my dress and pushed the driver out of his seat. That was when I smelled the alcohol. He reeked. So I told him that he had to give us our money back. He couldn't charge us for the ride. I drove us to the best place to watch the fireworks. We got there just in time. That was the first time your father proposed."

"Why didn't you tell me this before?" I ask. Dad is the family storyteller, and he's super talkative, but he's never spoken of this night.

"Because I said no," Mom said. "It wasn't practical. I wasn't ready to leave Russia. My babushka had just died. This was right after my mother got sick. My English was good, but I didn't know if I could live in such a different country. I couldn't leave my family. Not yet. Your father came back when my mother died, and that was when I said yes."

That's the story I know by heart, the one of Mom grieving, her second big loss. She doesn't count her father leaving when she was little. She doesn't remember him.

"You were a badass, Mom."

She smiles. A little proud. I sip the Prosecco, which bounces off my tongue, and find Mom staring at me. I gesture at my glass. "Nadine's idea."

"I wasn't looking at your glass. I was looking at you.

You're growing up to be a *krasivyy* girl." Beautiful. She holds my gaze. "It will be *strannyy* when you leave." Strange.

I'm a flower and she's the sun. I absorb her warmth and remind her, "I may not, remember?"

"It's impossible to predict the future," she says. "We don't know what the next few months will bring. You've done so well in school, and you could end up anywhere. How wonderful. We're very proud of you."

"If you go, you'll come home as much as you can," Tatya says. "Summer and holidays."

"We'll visit if you move away," Mom says.

I nearly choke on my Prosecco. I examine the food on the table to determine the exact ingredient that awoke my mother. When she raises that impenetrable wall, it feels like she's sleepwalking. You aren't supposed to wake a sleepwalker. It's unpredictable and even dangerous. Now, she sits before me, alert. The wall has crumbled down, just as it did in Berlin so many years ago. This moment feels as momentous.

"I'd love that," I say in a soft voice, hoping I won't scare her away.

"You know your dad wants you to go to NYU. I love New York," she says. "I'd love to visit Boston, too. I don't know much about this Rhode Island city, though. New York is the best choice, don't you think? Better than here. So much culture. The museums and opera. Perfect for your age. I hope you choose there."

My heart fills with dread. Is it possible that she *wants* me to move across the country? Maybe that would be easier for her—to have me far away so that when we're back together, she would have the ability to set her grief aside. Our visits would be like this meal, a stark contrast from our daily life as a family.

"Berkeley is nice and only across the bay. You know that's my top choice. And San Francisco has some of the best museums. I hate opera anyway," I say.

Mom asks, "Aren't you excited? Your father is giddy about all of your possibilities. I'm sure he's thinking about that right now—thinking about you and your future. He'll tell you that as soon as they find him. When he calls."

"Of course I'm excited, but it's hard thinking about college with the whole Dad-is-missing situation. We don't know when he's going to call, Mom." I stop myself from saying *if he's going to call.* So much for staying positive.

"You need to be strong," Tatya says. "Your mother is right. It helps to think about the future and all of the good things that will come. We need to stay hopeful. This is part of that."

"What if all of your friends go away?" Mom says, pressing on.

"I thought you wanted me to stay," I say.

Nadine nearly knocks over her glass when she reaches for my hand. "Of course we do."

I wait for Mom to say the same. "The world is big, Charlotte. You should see as much of it as you can. I'm glad I came here even though I was scared. Some things are more important than your home. Go have a *priklyucheniye*." An adventure. "That would be best." She breaks my gaze and sips her Prosecco.

"I have to go to the bathroom," I say. I don't want to cry at the table.

I close the door behind me and lower myself onto the bath mat, blinking away tears as I replay her words in my mind. I realize she didn't say it would be *sad* for me to leave, or *hard,* or *difficult.* She said it would be *strange*—not exactly a loving description. It would be *strange* if it snowed in San Francisco. It would be *strange* if dogs suddenly had the ability to speak. It would be *strange* if I declared myself a vegan. I want her to get misty-eyed and say it would be *heartbreaking* to have her only living child leave home, to see me only a couple of times a year. I want that absence to be as painful for her as it will be for me.

A knock at the door. "Charlotte," Tatya says.

I open it and Nadine squeezes in. "What are you doing on the floor?"

I shrug.

"She loves you."

I nod and feel more tears.

"She wants you to have the world. To have everything you want."

I think of my many long conversations with Emma, how we detail the great things about the cities we may call home. All of that excitement evaporates with the idea that Mom might want me to leave. I can't tell Nadine that all I need is my mother, so instead I ask, "Why isn't *she* telling me this? She didn't say anything like that at the table. Why isn't *she* in here?"

"She's serving the soup."

"Don't let me keep her from the *soup*. I know how important *soup* is."

She reaches down and pulls me to my feet. "You are the most important thing in the world to your parents. To me, too."

This is supposed to be our celebration dinner, and I'm ruining it by locking myself in the bathroom, but I can't face the idea that my departure could bring Mom relief, even peace. I wish Dad were here so I could ask him if this is true or if this is just a figment of my hypersensitive imagination. I hug Tatya.

When I let go, she holds my face in her hands and says,

"You're a wonderful girl. You are your parents' *serdtse*." Heart. "You know I was there after you were born. You should have seen your mother. You were sleeping on your mother's chest, and I held your hand. Your fingers were so small. When you woke up, you did something extraordinary. You kissed my hand. From the minute you were born, you were filled with so much love and tenderness. Your mom pulled you to her neck, to that soft spot." She taps her collarbone. "And you did the same thing. You gave her a kiss on the finger. You've never changed. You still love deeply. You show people that love. That's not so easy for your mother to do, but you need to understand that she loves nothing like she loves you. Absolutely nothing."

This makes me cry harder, but I manage to nod through my tears. "I'll be right out," I say.

Before she leaves, she kisses the top of my head. I wash my face and hope I can pull myself together enough to eat.

When I finally emerge, I'm startled to see Mom's red and swollen eyes. She doesn't look up when I sit down. Food fills our plates, and I pull the soup close and taste it. We have the habit of dipping Mom's bread into our soup, letting the crust absorb the warm broth. I reach for my plate and nearly gasp. When I look up, Mom's watching me with tears falling down her cheeks.

She's removed the slice of *kalach* and replaced it with an

enormous piece of black bread, which she's covered in deli-cate icing script that reads: *Gde by vy ni moye serdtse budet sledovat'*. Wherever you go my heart will follow.

Mom hands me the basket, and when she rests it on the table, she says, "It's too sweet to eat. Have some of the *kalach*." She covers my hand with hers, and I look at her fingers, the ones I kissed when I was freshly born.

I set the black bread aside and wonder if it's possible to somehow keep it fresh, to fight away the mold and prevent decomposition. I want to frame it and hang it above my bed like one of those cross-stitch doily things embroidered with greeting-card clichés. Now I understand why people adorn their walls with those sentimental verses. They're hanging on to moments like this, a reminder that even in the worst moments of doubt and despair, there can be a time of clarity, when your heart feels full with the fact that you're not alone. That even if you don't believe it at the time, even if you can't see it, you're totally and completely loved.

Ten

By morning, Mom's love message, the delicate words written in icing, has seeped into the bread, the words fading like a picture drawn on the bathroom mirror after a shower. A temporary image in the steam. I need to preserve last night beyond a memory. I blow through two rolls of film, one color and one black and white.

Tatya and Mom are busy in the bakery. Before school, I pop in for coffee and good-byes, and Mom's different. She doesn't stay in the kitchen. She doesn't offer her usual quick smile and wave, almost a dismissal. Now, she lingers behind the counter and asks about school. I tell her about my bio quiz, but not that I'm unprepared. I promise to come straight home this afternoon. I want to help. Mom suggests ordering takeout and watching a movie together. Unless I have too much homework. Unless I have plans with my friends. Whatever I want, she says. She looks me in the eye, not once glancing at her flour-covered hands.

The fog's so thick, it looks like it's still dark, and I drive through the empty parking lot close to the entrance, claiming one of the most coveted spots. I see a few teachers' cars, but all of the lights are on, the classrooms bright, the fluorescents combating the darkness outside. When I walk inside, though, the hallway is unlit, and I make my way through the shadows.

A certain sense of peace fills me in the darkroom, as though my body occupies the tray, becoming clearer the longer I stay in the solution. Photography is my meditation, my connection to the world. My camera demands me to see—really see—the details that fill the frame. When I develop pictures, especially portraits, faces peer at me through parting clouds. I stare into their eyes until I can see the color of their irises. The camera lens functions as an X-ray machine, allowing me to look inside someone and bring their feelings to the surface. From pressing the shutter release to hanging the finished print, I'm filled with a deep sense of appreciation. What if my parents hadn't given me a camera for my twelfth birthday?

Once I turn on the lights, it takes a second and several blinks to adjust. The drying photos are carefully pinned in a tidy line like my neighbor's clothes hung to dry in the sunlight. Even I, who second-guesses every formal photograph I snap, recognize their merit. I'd taken the pictures in a rush, wanting to get to school. Mom's faint words, which I worried would be too light to capture, are easy to read. But it's the composition, the way I hurriedly snapped the bread on the bare wood of Mom's well-worn butcher block. I hadn't given myself time to overthink. Not once did I fiddle with the placement of the bread, or even the lighting. The pictures appear rustic and at least fifty years old. I guess this is what timeless looks like.

Sometimes I feel as if I'm two different kinds of photographers: the one who takes photos like a journalist. The one Dad is so proud of. The one who filled out college applications for the schools with the best journalism programs. The one everyone expects me to be. And I want to be that, just like I want to be like Dad. Like Emma and Isaac and Megan. I love the news and I love being on the paper, but if I really, truly, seriously admitted it, that's not the kind of photographer I'd choose to be.

If I didn't have to think about parents and expectations and getting a job, I'd do something different. A lot of things. I'd take art classes and apply to art schools. I'd make collages and books, pages filled with portraits. I'd make more prints like I did during camp over spring break: digitally overlapping pictures to create something entirely new. I'd have a room like Josh's brother Ian, a gallery of images I created. Not beaches, though, but people.

That has to stay a hobby, though. Because I want to be

the same as Dad. I want to be part of the paper. I want to get a real job someday and travel and be paid to take pictures.

I love my time in the darkroom, how the peaceful blackness clears my head and opens my heart. That time needs to be contained, though, limited to developing film. Because however much I require my solitary creative moments, I also need my friends, and I need to be a member of something bigger. The Editorial Roundtable. My family. And now Josh.

Eleven

Just like on TV, I think, one agent fat, the other thin. Both bald and dressed in suits, similar to the one hanging in Dad's closet, bought begrudgingly on clearance from Men's Wearhouse. The third guy, young and wearing khakis rather than a suit, looks out of place. A sidekick or an intern or a curious bystander.

I came home to them sitting in the living room with Mom and Uncle Miguel. I don't know what was said before my arrival.

I don't want to know. It's clear that they're here with bad news. I want to turn around and run out of the apartment, and keep running until I pass out. Not this. Please not this.

I don't run, though. The tears are immediate and forceful, like waterfalls crashing down my cheeks.

Under her apron, Mom's still in yoga pants and Dad's shirt. The coffeepot gurgles in the kitchen. Uncle Miguel looks worse than before, even more haggard and stressed.

My stomach clenches, and no matter how hard I squeeze my eyes shut, the tears keep coming. They're relentless.

No one speaks. I look at Mom, who seems as anxious and confused and devastated as I am. I join her on the couch.

Uncle Miguel introduces the men as agents from the FBI. Their names are long and forgettable. I want to cover their mouths to prevent them from speaking. I want to scream so loud that I shatter every window and piece of glass in the house.

"Please," Mom says, her accent thicker than usual, the telltale sign that she's nervous. "Go on." Aside from her clothes and accent, Mom seems composed. She offers coffee, and the men shake their heads. The thin man shifts in his seat. The young one stares.

Uncle Miguel meets my eyes, and I'm unprepared for his expression: hopeless and distraught. I clench my fists. I want to hear the news from him, not these strange men who should climb back into my TV and continue acting in some stupid crime show. They can't be real. They can't be here. They can't know Dad's name or whereabouts or fate.

"Tell me," I say to Uncle Miguel. If I ignore the men, maybe they'll disappear.

When Mom grabs my hand, she's not tender, she holds it too tight, like she wants this to stop, for everyone to stay silent.

I feel her pulse as she squeezes harder. Now I sense the depth of her grief. It's like she yanked out her heart, fuller than I ever feared, and put it in my hand. It's almost too heavy to hold. She releases her grip, and my palm is blotched red and white where her fingers were. She crosses her legs and scoots over, and I know she's gone. She's climbed back inside herself.

"Please tell Charlotte what's going on." Her voice sounds steadier now, clear, like she's lived in this country longer than twenty years.

When the round man speaks, I see that he has a kind face, that he doesn't want to be here either. "I'm sorry to have to tell you this, but your father has been abducted. We're doing everything we can to free them."

"Him and Pascal Baudin," I say.

The agents look startled. "How do you know that?" They stare at me like I'm an animal with a magical ability to speak.

I know better than to divulge Megan's investigative news assignment. I nod in Miguel's direction. "He told me when Dad went missing."

"Listen to me," the round one says. "It is critical that you don't mention your father and Mr. Baudin to anyone. That's very important. *No one* must know that your dad is missing. Do you understand?"

"My friends know. I filled them in at school."

The agents look at one another, and the tall one speaks.

"Don't discuss it further. Don't tell anyone new, especially adults. If your friends ask, you can say that the newspaper has some leads. Everything is under control."

"But it isn't," I say, looking at the agents, daring them to contradict me. Miguel takes the empty seat next to me. I can barely look at him after I realize he's been crying.

"Lottie, if your friends ask, deflect everything back to me," Uncle Miguel says. "The government is working on bringing your dad home. Hopefully, this will be over soon."

"How do you know he's been taken?" I ask, ignoring the agents, focusing only on Uncle Miguel. One, I'll know if he's holding back. Two, I'll sense if he's lying. I've watched him and Dad play cards my entire life. I can tell when he's bluffing— even before Dad can. He pushes up his glasses with his index finger, an ordinary gesture, but one he always does when drawing a disappointing card.

He smiles and shakes his head. "They actually called me."

"Mr. Rodriguez, we're going to ask you to stop there," the round one says.

Mom sits up in her seat. "We have a right to know everything that you've told Miguel. What are you doing in Ukraine? *Vy govorite Ukrainskiy?* Do you speak Ukrainian?"

At the sound of Russian, the agents exchange another look. "We have people on the ground," the tall one says.

It doesn't matter what she's wearing. When Mom sits

with her ballet spine, her head still, her eyes clear, everyone pays attention. Yes, she's beautiful, but what they really react to is this. Her presence. It's the strangest combination of poise and fragility. I don't know how else to describe it. Nadine says it's a sign of someone who was once very strong and then broke, shattered inside, which is what happened when my sister died and Mom had her stroke.

I don't want this porcelain-doll Mom. I want the Mom from the other night, the one who watched two sci-fi movies with me. The one who polished off a dozen cookies. The one who made me believe we might get through this.

The agents sit attentively while Mom details her family tree, relatives in St. Petersburg, a cousin in government. The agents look intimidated and impressed. The tall one takes notes. The sidekick stays quiet, and he hasn't looked at anyone but me and Mom.

"Why did they call you?" I ask Uncle Miguel. "And not Mom or the government? What do they want?"

He takes a deep breath and pauses. I notice that he doesn't look at the agents, just at me, and I understand that Uncle Miguel won't hide anything. I'll hound him until I know every last detail. I'm like Dad that way.

"They have demands," he says. "Ransom and other things. They want the newspaper to pay. They want publicity for their cause."

"Which is?" I ask.

"They want to be a part of Russia," Uncle Miguel says. "Not Ukraine. Like most wars, they're fighting over land."

The tall agent shakes his head. "Mr. Rodriguez—"

"He's talking to me," I say. "That's good about the ransom, right?" I look at everyone in the room. "Just pay it."

The round one looks at me like I'm a kindergartener, and the urge to scream returns.

"The United States does not negotiate with terrorists. I'm sorry. I know this is hard to hear, but there will be no ransom. We're doing everything we can to bring your father home. This is Raj Singh. He is a family liaison and will be your contact going forward. He'll keep you informed of all developments. You can call him anytime. Know that this is a priority."

Raj Singh leans forward, places his business card on the table, and shakes our hands. He can't be that much older than me—midtwenties, tops. He looks younger than Megan. With his perfectly combed dark hair and perfectly square jaw and perfectly long and proportioned nose, he looks like a prom king. Someone who belongs on a college campus rather than in my living room. I wonder if this is his first job. If we're his first case.

"I don't care what the policy is. Just pay the ransom," I say. I want to sound strong, but it comes out a little desperate, a little pleading. "Bring my dad home."

The agents shake their heads in unison. They're choreographed in their movements, well rehearsed in disappointing the powerless.

This time, it's Uncle Miguel who takes my hand. I don't ask any more questions of the agents, knowing they'll give vague answers. I'll save them for him.

Twelve

Mom's in the kitchen. She faces me, and I see that she's in a whirlpool of grief. Her eyes are so swollen, she looks like she flew through a windshield. She pulls another loaf of *kalach* from the oven. It warms my hand, and I realize I'm freezing. Goose bumps line my skin, and I feel so shaken that my teeth might chatter. I need something to ground me, but Mom is too unhinged to help.

"What are you going to do now?" I ask after taking a bite. I want the flavor to comfort me like usual, but it doesn't. I barely taste it.

"I need to make some phone calls. My cousin is going to try to get information."

"Viktor?" I ask. I've never been to Russia—I've never even seen snow—but I am familiar with Mom's family tree. Only her sister, Tatya Rayna, visits, and she hasn't been here since freshman year. "I thought he was in the agriculture department."

"Government is government," she says. "He knows people." Mom furrows her brow, a relief, because it makes her look serious, which is close enough to looking strong. "Why don't you go for that run? Running always makes you feel better."

"Now?" I ask. At first, I'm hurt, and then I see the tears stockpiled behind her lashes and understand that she needs the apartment to herself.

"Okay," I say. "I'll be back soon."

Before traveling, it's good luck to sit for a minute and quietly prepare for a journey. Dad never did this, and although I'm only going to the beach, I close my door and rest on my bed. It is a gift for Mom, along with my absence.

When I walk past her in the kitchen, she's facing the sink and window, head bent, crying. I want to stay. I'd do anything to comfort her. To feel less alone.

I go downstairs and into the bakery. Tatya Nadine sits behind the counter. I don't know who needs her more: Mom or me.

"Will you check on her in a little while?" I ask. "I don't know what to do."

"Come here, *moya lyubov'*." My love. When she wraps her arms around me, I allow myself to cry—really cry.

"I feel like I'm losing her, too," I say. "She's going to stop talking again. I know it."

Nadine shakes her head. "No, that won't happen. I know your mother. She's stronger now. Nothing is like losing a child. And you can't give up hope. Your father is alive. He'll come home."

I cling to her, holding even tighter, worrying I'll bruise her plump arms. Tatya Nadine knows Mom better than anyone, maybe even Dad. She nursed Mom after my sister died and then again when I almost killed her.

Lena died of crib death at eleven months old. Mom had me a year later, way too soon, according to her doctor. I don't know much, hardly any details. Just how long she labored to have me, the emergency cesarean section, a staggering amount of lost blood. And then, after I was born, how the preeclampsia caused her blood pressure to soar, setting off a stroke that almost took her from us forever.

The first time Mom stopped speaking—not a word for two and a half months—was after Lena died. Then she became pregnant with me and her voice returned. The second was for four months after I was born, the first sixteen weeks of my life. I entered the world without hearing her voice, coos, lullabies. Nothing but her heartbeat and tears.

They blamed the stroke. I blame myself.

I've heard bits and pieces of the story, of Mom's grief, of her periods of silence. I've overheard more—hushed phone calls to her sister in Russia, whispered confessions. That part of her wishes she had died instead of surviving the stroke. That sometimes she can't bear to look at me without seeing my dead sister. She worries I was born with a curse, that I was born a *potercha,* the troubled spirit of a dead child who takes the form of a blackbird that summons lightning and storms. When a blackbird rests on a windowsill, Mom leaves the room, pale-faced and unwilling to meet my eyes.

Sometimes Mom drinks too much wine before she calls her sister. Sometimes she isn't as quiet as she intends.

While Mom worries that I'm a *potercha,* I wonder if she's *Umershey Materi.* The Dead Mother.

A long time ago in some Russian peasant village, a couple had a baby boy, but the wife wasn't as lucky as Mom. She died in childbirth, and the baby was left both motherless and hungry. He wouldn't drink from anyone else. The father was wrecked at the thought of also losing his son.

Desperate, he hired an old nanny to help take care of his baby, who still wouldn't drink and cried all day long. They tried everything to get him to drink water or cow's milk. Nothing worked. But the baby slept through the night.

Even though the baby cried all day long, he plumped up; he wasn't dying of starvation. After several more peaceful nights, the father and nanny freaked out.

When the baby went to sleep, both of them huddled on the nursery floor. They heard the door creak open and saw a shadowed figure approach the cradle. She lifted the baby to her chest. He cooed and cuddled. Through the darkness, the father and nanny tried to identify the woman, but it was too dark to see. They speculated about who this mystery woman might be. Why did she come in secret? If she was a wet nurse, couldn't she help during the day? She was saving the baby's life, but her secrecy scared the hell out of them.

The next night, the nanny had the idea of placing a candle near the crib. Right on time, the door opened at midnight, and they saw her, the baby's dead mother dressed in her burial clothes. She held the baby as he nursed, only now the father and nanny understood that he drank from a dead woman. They could see her face, her features still clear, and recognized her bittersweet smile and expression of a love that transcends death.

Who knew how long she would have come. Weeks? Months? Years? Maybe, only in moonlight, she would have taken care of him throughout his childhood. But they would never know, because as soon as the candlelight revealed the ghost mother, she vanished with a look of anguish worse than death. The father rushed to the cradle, ready to comfort his son, but as he lifted him up, he saw that the baby was dead.

Part of Mom died with Lena, as though our mother continues to care for her beyond the grave. I can't imagine what it must have been like for her to dress me in Lena's clothes, wrap me in her blankets, and lower me into Lena's crib every night. The thought splits my soul in two.

I want to measure her heart, see if it's reached capacity. How much grief can Mom endure? First Lena. Maybe Dad. Am I enough, her *potercha*? Or will I always remind her of what she's lost?

I don't tell Tatya Nadine any of this. I don't dare. Some things shouldn't be spoken out loud. I learned that the hard way.

I let her hold me, grateful for her like I've never been. When she lets go, I ask her to go upstairs and check on Mom.

I don't run. I walk to the tulip garden, wishing the flowers had kept blooming for me. But I know wishes are nothing but fantasy. Something to cling to when everything is hard. When it feels like nothing will ever get better.

I remember Megan's words again. *Be positive.*

Dad is alive. He isn't trapped beneath ten stories of bricks. The United States government regards his return as a priority.

Vozvrashchat'sya, Dad. Come back.

Thirteen

Deciding I need the exercise, I sprint home. My feet pound the asphalt, and I run faster than I have in all my cross-country years. *Stay positive. Come home.*

Mom and I will get through this together. We'll watch hours of movies. We'll eat a staggering amount of baked goods. We'll polish off the rest of Dad's lasagna and we'll order Chinese. We'll hunker down and wait for Raj Singh, FBI Family Liaison.

Dad will come home.

The apartment door is unlocked again, and I bound in, eager to reassure Mom. I'm filled with adrenaline and hope. I find her at the kitchen table, alone, drinking a mug of tea. She looks worse than before, puffy and swollen from crying.

"Good. You're back. That was a long run. You were gone for a couple of hours. Are you hungry?" She rises and picks up a plate, filling it with apple strudel.

I accept the food and take a bite. "Where's Tatya?" I ask.

"I sent her home so I could sleep, only I couldn't sleep," she says, smiling weakly. "But I'm going to try again now that you're here." Mom squeezes my shoulder as she leaves the room. I listen as she walks down the hallway, her faint footsteps disappearing when she shuts her bedroom door.

Once, grief claimed my mother and left me with a ghost. Please don't steal her from me again.

The last thing I want to do is sit alone in the living room, so I copy Mom and sequester myself away. We're in a prison or a convent or some other confined place, cut off from each other. Maybe cut off from everything. Only I leave my door open—an invitation in case she ventures out. I wish she'd do the same.

My room is a tornado-worthy disaster. Dirty clothes and stacks of books and paper everywhere. Funnel-cloud-level damage. When did I rip my comforter? Then I see the stray pair of scissors used for my last collage.

I'd returned the scattered photos of Dad to the box, but I couldn't bring myself to tuck them away in the closet. Especially not now. I need him close, and his portrait is all I have.

About a dozen containers are strewn across the floor just waiting to be tripped over. When I lift the lid of an untouched carton, I spot the prints from our Hawaii vacation last year.

Mom and Dad in scuba gear. So many sunsets and sea turtles.

Then I see the ones from the volcano. My daredevil father too close to the edge. I swear Mom almost died of a heart attack. She actually got mad at him—really, really angry—because he wouldn't listen. She called him a child and huffed to the car. It took him ten minutes to coax her back out.

Dad's kind of clueless. It took him a few minutes to realize Mom was genuinely pissed. And in those minutes, the sky deepened to tangerine and crimson and prom-dress pink. The kind of sunset reserved for wall calendars and postcards. My goofy father raised his hands to the sky like he had painted those colors himself. I snapped and snapped and snapped, and every one of those pictures turned out perfectly. Too bad Mom was glaring at him from the rental car.

That's when I remember Mom's book of Russian folktales. I pull it down and run my hand over the gold cover, flipping through the pages until I find it. *Zsharptitsa.* The Firebird, whose eyes sparkle like jewels and whose feathers are the same colors as that Hawaiian sunset. The Firebird's song heals the sick, curing the most serious diseases, even blindness. In the middle of the night, *Zsharptitsa* flies through the sky, so magical that one single feather can illuminate a dark room. When it stretches its wings, it outshines the brightest star.

It isn't a good omen—it's the best damn omen in the world.

Old bio quizzes and English papers cover my printer. I sweep them all to the floor. I scan the ornate illustrations in the book and then the photos of Dad in Hawaii.

I haven't played with this technique since camp. It takes a few tries before I remember how to overlap the images, layering Dad and the Firebird. At first, the color is all wrong and it looks like a kindergartner's attempt at Photoshop. When I fiddle with the saturation, the images blend together, like Dad and the bird share the same sky. Finally, it works.

I press print and wait for the thick photo paper to emerge.

There he is, Dad, smiling with arms raised to the sky, to the Firebird, which soars above him, almost celestial. The Firebird keeping him safe. *Zsharptitsa* will bring him home.

Fourteen

Mom picks the strangest moments to act like a regular, engaged mother. I want to stay home from school. An understandable desire given that the alternative is spending the day keeping this secret, staying quiet as my friends relentlessly ask for updates. Mom insists, though. She even packs me lunch.

There's no way in hell I'm going. Emma and Isaac will sense something's up—they're like dogs that way—and get the truth out of me. Then I'd need to keep them quiet. Impossible.

I've never skipped school before. Mom and Dad let me stay home whenever I said I didn't feel well, not something Mom is likely to do now.

Mom gives me a listless hug. Once I'm in Dad's car, I text Josh asking if he'd be up for a day of not talking. Does he want to see the Diane Arbus photography exhibit at SFMOMA? How invested is he in his attendance record?

He replies quickly.

Yes. Maybe. Not at all.

I pick him up a half hour later. Josh lives in Presidio Heights. The car strains up what feels like the steepest incline in the city, and I circle the block three times looking for his house.

Tucked between two enormous quasi-mansions sits a small stucco house out of place in the opulent neighborhood, a pebble among boulders.

I knock three times before he opens the door. He's out of breath. "Sorry," he says. "I was on the phone with my brother. He's calling in my absence. I can always count on him to cover for me. He's saved my ass on several occasions."

Josh smiles and ushers me in. I take in the mishmash of styles. Old antiwar protest posters hang above elegant antique furniture, the kind on display at the Palace of Fine Arts. A tapestry covers a chair, but it doesn't fully cover the intricately carved wood and velvet cushion. It's part Haight-Ashbury hippie apartment and part Pacific Heights formal parlor.

He watches me take it in. "This was my grandparents' house. It was never supposed to stay. They built a bunch of bungalows after the 1906 earthquake. Most of them got torn down. My parents don't believe in throwing stuff away— good furniture, anyway. So they kept all of my grandparents' stuff. But they're Berkeley people, you know, activists. My dad calls it 'intergenerational decorating.' My room is all IKEA, though."

I blush at the mention of his bedroom.

"So, you going to tell me what's going on? Why you're skipping school for the first time?"

"How do you know it's my first time?"

"Let's just say I'm observant." He gives me a smile, and I find myself relaxing even though I've had all of my muscles clenched for hours. Even though I barely slept again. Even though I can't believe I'm standing in the middle of Josh's living room.

"It's got to be a nontalking day," I say.

"Sworn to secrecy?"

I nod.

"On a scale from one to ten, with ten being the worst possible thing in the world, what number?"

I take a deep breath. Ten would be that Dad died. Nine would be that he's seriously hurt. "Eight," I say. "But it feels like ten."

Josh takes a step closer and wraps his arms around me. "We can be mute if you want. We can be mimes or something."

When he kisses me, his lips taste of toothpaste and sugar, a perfect sweetness as though I had just pulled him from the oven. My mind empties until he's the primary thought in my head. I trace the length of his arm with my fingernails, pleased when goose bumps rise to the surface of his skin. His lips leave mine, and when he moves his to my neck, I gently push him away. If I don't stop now, we'll be on the couch for the next hour. Too much too soon.

"You're addictive," I say, resting my head against his chest, lulled by the rise and fall of his breath.

He kisses my neck again, this time sweetly rather than urgently. "I could stay like this all day."

I laugh. "That's the problem."

"Let's go outside," he says. "I want to show you something."

A breeze blows the curls away from my face as we are greeted by a symphony of bells and the scent of gardenia bushes. "What's that sound?" I ask.

"My grandma's wind garden."

I follow him along a stone path that opens to large garden, something completely unexpected. We're surrounded by flowers. Every kind imaginable.

"In a couple of months, her roses will bloom," Josh says. "I used to play here before she died. We lived in Berkeley back then. She collected them for smell, so it's like stepping into a perfume bottle. I used to sit out here and draw while she pulled weeds and stuff. She practically lived out here. You should see it in the summer. You'll have to come and take pictures."

It's habitual the way I compose a shot as soon as I walk into a new place, as though that's how I make it real. My camera anchors me, allowing me to absorb the new environment. I close my eyes for a second and listen to the wind chimes. "It's really beautiful," I say.

"When I was old enough, I started buying wind chimes for her birthday and Christmas. Sometimes just because. I went all over. The shells are from Half Moon Bay, and the bamboo ones are from Japantown, and the tiny bells are from an Indian bazaar in Oakland. There's a big trellis near the gate that's covered with wisteria, and I hung a bunch of chimes there."

"Can you show me?"

Josh rattles off the plants as we go: French lavender, jasmine, California poppies, African irises, and dormant roses. We walk under a giant angel's trumpet with dangling blooms, which dust us in blessing.

"Do you take care of the garden now?"

"Hell no. My parents do it. Here," he says when we're under the trellis, "raise your arms as high as you can."

I can barely reach the chimes on tiptoe. I gasp when he places his hands on my hips to help me up. I rest my body against his as my fingers touch the bells, one by one, creating the sweetest notes. I close my eyes and move my hands back and forth, hitting high and low notes, playing my own jumbled melody. As I play, the trellis quivers, sending down wisteria petals that fall onto my hair.

"I feel like a kobzar."

"What's that?" Josh lowers me back to the ground

"There's an old Russian stringed instrument, kinda like a lute, called a *bandura*. Musicians who played it were called *bandurists*. Some of them were blind, and eventually, most of them were. It became a really strange tradition. I guess if you went blind, they gave you a *bandura*. They even had a special name—a blind *bandurist* was called a *kobzar*. If I close my eyes, I'm a wind chime *kobzar*."

"That's cool in a weird way. I thought you'd love this. I've been wanting to bring you out here for a while."

"I'm glad you did." I'm almost surprised when I smile. Missing Dad is all-consuming, and the anxiety is getting to be overwhelming. "I get so caught up in what's happening with my dad. It's hard not to be totally and completely hope-less. I don't feel that way right now. It's not like that when I'm with you." I feel the smile still on my face. He does that to me—makes everything light and giddy. The chimes continue to play in harmony, with the wind as the conductor.

"It's different, but I know what it's like to be cut off from everything," he says. "One day life's boring, but a good boring. Then everything changes in an instant, like a cab-driver turning the wrong way onto a one-way street. Boom.

My grandparents are dead. Life's never going to be the same. When they died, I stopped caring as much. I still think about the important stuff, you know, like grades and wanting to make films. But I stopped caring about what people think of me. I want to make movies, and I want to do something good. And I want to be with you."

Josh touches my face, the outline of my lips, before pulling me close for a kiss. I feel him everywhere: my mouth and my neck. When we pull apart, out of breath and covered in wisteria petals, I say, "Me too."

We never make it to the museum. Josh says he likes moving pictures more than still ones, and we debate the finer points of photography versus film. His room is covered with framed movie posters: Fellini, Hitchcock, Wes Anderson, Coppola, and Tarantino. He's both shocked and disgusted that I've never seen a Hitchcock film, so we climb onto his bed and stream *Vertigo* and then *North by Northwest.* We behave. We don't go too far, even though part of me wants to. It doesn't matter how long we've liked each other. I can't be with him that way while Dad is missing. I want to be with Josh because I want to be with *him,* not because I'm using him as anesthesia to numb the pain.

Fifteen

I try to pull open the door to the bakery, but it doesn't move.
Locked. The store empty and dark.

Tatya and Mom wouldn't abandon the shop unless something terrible happened. One of them would be sweeping or mopping or stocking or prepping.

I take the stairs to the apartment two at a time, freezing the second I hear Raj Singh's voice.

They sit in a circle: Raj Singh, Mom, Tatya Nadine, and Uncle Miguel. With the exception of Raj, who looks like he's the hostage, the rest look frustrated. Mom looks plain mad, glaring at Raj the same way she glared at me after discovering my empty bed back when I was going out with Kyle.

Mom's eyes are dry—no tears or smudged raccoon eyeliner. Tatya Nadine's generous application of foundation remains intact.

It's like my day with Josh never happened, the hours of

relaxed muscles and a clear head. I look at them, guessing what could be wrong, but I can't even think clearly. All of this is too much. I miss Dad. I need Dad. He's the only person who can get me through this, and he's gone. It hits me hard, so hard that I double over—the fact that he may be gone for good. Whoever said feelings can't kill you was full of it.

Uncle Miguel rises and folds me into his arms, but it's Mom who speaks, just glancing at me for a second before returning her impressive stink eye to Raj.

"They freed Pascal. France paid the ransom. But"—Mom points at Raj, her arm a perfect line from ballet and yoga—"he's refusing to do the same for your father. They're leaving him there to die."

Her voice rises with each word.

Raj Singh crosses his legs and looks painfully uncomfortable. He shifts again like he has a full bladder—or something worse. "Mrs. Lang—"

"You can call me Valentina." She's calm, but she possesses an angry stillness that gives even me chills. Hello again, badass Mom, who took over a motorboat in the middle of the Neva River. It's nice to see you.

"I'm getting a beer," Uncle Miguel says. He shoots Raj an impatient look, also in the stink eye category, and leaves the room. I follow him into the kitchen.

"How did you find out?" I ask.

"The rebels released a video. It hasn't hit the media yet. I give it an hour, tops."

I storm into the living room, suddenly as angry as Mom, and tap at the closed laptop resting on the coffee table. "Show me."

Raj searches my face, probably gauging how much of Mom's temper I've inherited.

"Play the video," I say. "Please."

Uncle Miguel reaches over me, opening the screen and pressing a few keys. Pascal speaks in heavily accented English. He expresses his gratitude to Mother Russia and support of the rebels' goal of annexing the region. He says the United States must follow France if we ever want to see Jeremiah Lang again.

When I lean close, my breath clouding the screen, I see Pasqual's exposed arms, his face. One bruise on his temple. That's it. He looks clean, even. Maybe they are gentle terrorists, not ones to hurt and torture. Maybe Dad isn't injured. Captive but unharmed.

Mom and I meet eyes, and I understand her anger, fully, like she gave me a transfusion and fury pumps through my veins. I welcome it. It's such a relief to feel angry because fury makes me feel stronger.

"What are you doing to bring my dad home?" I ask Raj. "You're supposed to be our liaison, but you haven't told us a single thing. You haven't done a damn thing."

Tatya Nadine puts her hand on my arm. "Shh, Charlotte. You don't need to yell."

I shake my arm free. "They need to do something!" I say. As quickly as I felt the anger, now I feel the tears. Gone are my few seconds of strength. That won't stop me.

I turn to Raj. "I don't care that you're working hard. I don't care that the damn president has been briefed. I care that my dad is locked up somewhere while this guy is fine and is getting released. So if you guys can't do your job, maybe you should let us do it."

Mom speaks in the politest tone of voice ever used by humankind. They should record her and send it to the United Nations. But I know that, just like me, she's fighting the urge to scream for them to bring my father home. "We want a better sense of what you're doing diplomatically and militarily. If you're asking us to have confidence in you, we need to understand how you're working on this. I've been talking to my family every day. They have resources. Maybe we should fly to Russia and see how we can help."

Tatya Nadine nods. "I'm visiting family next month. I can change my ticket and go earlier."

Uncle Miguel takes a swig of beer and chuckles. "And I run the front page of one of the biggest newspapers in the country. I can put whatever I want on it."

I want to laugh as I spot his telltale tic. He's bluffing. I've never loved him more than I do right now.

I don't think I'm imagining it when I see Raj gaze longingly at Uncle Miguel's beer.

Mom, Tatya Nadine, Uncle Miguel, and I wait. A tribunal.

Raj, obviously nervous, shifts again before speaking. "We've identified the key leaders in the group." He looks at each of us. "I said they're new, and they are, but their ties to established organizations are strong. Their network has grown, and they're linked to the faction that shot down that passenger jet and is responsible for the recent bombings. The people who are holding Jeremiah are loosely affiliated and much lower-level. We don't know how experienced they are, but we do know they are in touch with the aggressive group."

He looks at us again, like he's deciding how serious we are about trying to take things into our own hands. "This is a delicate situation. We're trying to determine how to approach this without fully engaging the larger rebel group. If you interfere, you could jeopardize everything. If you publish anything, you could jeopardize everything. You need to do as we say if we're going to have any chance of saving Jeremiah."

"Then pay the ransom," I say. "Because if you don't, maybe we'll have to figure out how to bring him home on our own. You know we have connections in Russia."

Maybe because I'm the only kid in the room, he stares at me when he responds. "If you interfere, we'll be forced to confiscate your passports. You can't fly to Russia right now and take things into your own hands. The United States doesn't negotiate with terrorists. You're U.S. citizens. This applies to you regardless of your family in Russia."

Everyone falls silent, so silent that our breathing is the loudest sound in the room. Mom stares at her hands, Tatya at her lap, Uncle Miguel at his beer.

Raj continues to look at each of us, gaining confidence, straightening his spine. The restless shifting stops.

Uncle Miguel is the one to break the silence. "What have you learned from Pascal?"

"It's too soon to know," Raj says. "He's in transit now. We're working closely with France, and after we interview him, we hope to be able to pinpoint Jeremiah's exact location so we can attempt a rescue. I can't give you any more information than that. Remember, you have to be discreet. We have to control the public narrative." He leans forward, elbows resting on knees. "I need to say this again. I know you're scared and I see you're frustrated, but you cannot interfere, regardless of your contacts in Russia. It's against the law. It's treason."

"So, what do we do now?" I ask. "Since you don't really have anything to tell us and we're not allowed to do anything."

"There's nothing to do but wait," he says. "Keep to your-selves. Be discreet and don't discuss the situation outside of the four of you. Hopefully, we'll have good news soon."

Uncle Miguel's phone begins to beep in rapid succession. A news alert flashes across my phone.

"Turn on the TV," Uncle Miguel says.

Pascal's face fills the screen, with the ticker at the bottom announcing his release. I flip the channel. It airs on all of the cable news stations. We sit and watch as they play the video in full, then clips as they dissect his words. On the big screen, I notice that what I thought was a bruise looks more like dirt. He needs a shower, not medical attention. That's the only relief. I flinch when I see a photo of Dad on the screen. The ticker reads JEREMIAH LANG TAKEN HOSTAGE ONE WEEK AGO.

Sixteen

I barely recognize Dad, who, in the video, wears a moth-brown jumpsuit, too short to cover his long limbs. I fixate on his bony wrists and ankles. Bruises of every shade cover his skin. Violet and yellow and aubergine, the entire color spectrum.

I haven't allowed myself to think of the details of his captivity, of locked doors and men with guns. Now, though, I imagine everything, and it's like I'm trapped inside a *matryoshka* doll. I feel like the smallest of the nesting dolls, the tiny one in the center, buried within layers of larger hollow figurines.

The video is everywhere: first YouTube and cable news. Now network TV and all of the news sites. Mom and I sit in front of the TV while Uncle Miguel talks on his phone with someone from the FBI. Not Raj.

Just a couple of hours after Pascal's release video went public, Uncle Miguel received an email at work. A link to this video. Now the rebels want more money and a prisoner exchange. Raj is due to return any minute.

I keep waiting for Mom to speak, but she hasn't said a word since Uncle Miguel came back. Tatya Nadine stayed with us. She's keeping watch on Mom.

I turned off my phone. Everyone keeps texting, and even though I couldn't care less about Raj's order to be discreet, I can't imagine talking right now. I catch my breath at the thought. I've never been this scared in my life. I stare at my hands, at my legs, but have a hard time feeling them. The first time I saw the video, I felt like I hovered above my body, part ghost, as I listened to Dad speak. I barely feel human.

I try to ground myself by watching the video over and over, looking for clues, reminding myself that Dad's still alive.

It's hard to focus. I keep playing the video on my laptop, staring at Dad's face, listening to his hoarse voice saying his name, that he is a journalist, that he is an American. He sits cross-legged, and even though it's only been a week, his hair looks longer. Maybe that's because his head is bent down. They have to poke him with a rifle to get him to look into the camera.

The video is forty-nine seconds long. I've watched it sixty-one times. I keep expecting Mom to take my laptop away, but it appears she's no longer communicating with the living. She sits straight and still, eyes glued to the TV, without looking my way.

In the video, I can't see the gray in Dad's dark salt-and-pepper hair or the scar on his hand from the time he changed a tire on the Bay Bridge. The room he's in is dark and the film grainy. A twin mattress rests on the floor, covered with a thin beige blanket, but no sheets. Or pillow. This is what I focus on—Dad's lack of a pillow and sheets. It's easier than dissecting the rainbow of bruises.

I can't tell if the dark spots on his chin are scabs or stubble. Dad is capable of growing a full beard in a handful of days. He's insanely hairy. Sometimes I call him Sasquatch.

Uncle Miguel hangs up the phone, and I observe Mom to see if she notices. She doesn't appear to.

"They're interviewing Pascal now," he says, putting his arm around me. "Do me a favor and stop watching that." He taps my laptop.

"Now what?" I ask.

"We'll learn more from Raj. He's going into a briefing and will call back as soon as he's done. Valentina?" He walks over to Mom and places his hand on her arm. "Valentina?"

She jumps in her seat. She hasn't slept in two nights, and she's still wearing Dad's shirt.

"Valentina," Uncle Miguel says. "Why don't you take a shower, and we'll make some coffee."

Mom stands and looks my way like she just realized I'm here. "Charlotte, will you call Nadine and tell her she doesn't need to come back. We'll see her in the morning."

Uncle Miguel follows me into the kitchen and watches as I heat some bread in the oven. He knows the kitchen as well as I do, so he busies himself with filling the coffeepot. I guess he decided to stop drinking beer. I wish I could have one instead of coffee. Anything to make me feel calm. Anything to temper the tension running throughout my body. One minute I'm tense, and then I'm numb.

Uncle Miguel pats my arm. "I've seen your mom like this before. She just needs a good night's sleep and she'll be better. Don't worry."

"Okay," I say. I don't tell him that I'm concerned that my mother will become catatonic by day's end. That people shouldn't be capable of sitting so still for so long.

"You doing okay?" he asks.

"Aside from the whole video of some asshole holding a gun to my dad's head? Sure, great!"

"Lottie." He stops after saying my name and pulls me into a bear hug. He must sense how lost I am without Dad. When I close my eyes, I pretend Uncle Miguel is him.

"Are they going to save him?" I ask, my voice so quiet, I'm not sure if I said the words out loud.

He holds me tighter. "I hope so."

"I need you to do something," I say as I wipe my cheeks. He steps back so he can look at me. "What?"

"You need to tell me everything. Don't try to protect me, because I'll find out in the end. I'm old enough to know what's going on. I don't want you and Mom to keep things from me."

He crosses his arms and nods slowly. "Okay. You're going to hear a lot of conflicting stuff on the news—and a lot of things that are completely false. Don't panic. I'll make sure you know what's really happening. Okay?"

"Yes. Thanks," I say. "I mean it."

"You know how proud of you your dad is, right? I want you to hold on to that. I know the video is hard to see, but it is a good sign. We can see that he hasn't been harmed—"

"He's covered in bruises!" I say.

"I know, Lottie, but he's alive. He can talk. He can sit upright. These are all very good things. And now the FBI has a visual of where he's being held. They're analyzing it now."

"You sound like you think they're doing a good job."

Uncle Miguel shakes his head. "I think they're doing the best they can. I don't think we should just sit back and wait, though."

"What are you going to run in the paper?" I ask.

"I'm not sure yet. I'm not calling the shots like I usually do. The FBI is talking with the publisher, and I'm being told what I can and can't do. Right now, we're running stuff off the AP wire. They want us to play it safe so the rebels will stay in touch with the paper."

I can see the TV from the kitchen. Dad's image flashes across the muted screen, and I realize that to everyone else, he's just another story. One more event in an endless list of tragedies. I stare at the picture, at Dad's empty eyes, and I wonder how long people will pay attention.

Seventeen

The next morning, a parade of well-meaning visitors appears at the door, old ladies from the neighborhood and youngish women from the cultural center, ones who enroll in Mom's cooking classes in the hopes of winning men's hearts with perfectly baked treats. All morning, and then well into the afternoon, they offer condolences and food meant to comfort the grieving. Dishes that make my stomach turn.

I want to turn them away and explain that Dad isn't dead. He's captive, bruised, and maybe wounded—but alive. Instead, I invite them inside the apartment. Ask them to sit. Habitually, I offer pastries and coffee. I guess in some ways, I am my mother's daughter. They are kind, especially after I explain that Mom is unavailable, either holed up in her room or baking downstairs. They tell me to take care of my mother. To focus on my studies. To stay strong.

Nadine is the only one who can coax Mom out of the apartment, and then only to work.

I leave the funeral dishes, untouched, on the counter.

Emma, Isaac, and Josh text hourly, and I respond with three words: Can't talk now.

Without Dad, the apartment feels too large, almost vast. Once again, I understand Mom's impulse to cocoon in her room. When the visitors taper off late in the afternoon, I lower the blinds in my bedroom and pull the boxes of photos from my closet, arranging stacks of prints on my bed.

One by one, I add more photos of Dad to my collaged door, and then my already crowded wall, covering my friends with vacation snapshots. Pictures taken at the Eiffel Tower and Empire State Building and Space Needle. They'll understand.

Dad always smiles in photos, and he tickles and prods Mom to do the same. She's not naturally sour and scowling, but she's serious and poised. Perfect posture. When she's not in the kitchen or bakery, she wears her hair down, hanging just past her shoulders. I have Dad's curls and dark hair. Mom's is straight and lighter, almost auburn, with streaks of gold. Her eyes are a startling pale blue, like mine. When she was little, classmates accused her of having ghost eyes. Her pale skin and unnerving quiet only contributed to her mysteriousness. Mom often says that if she lived centuries ago, she likely would have been accused of being a witch and set aflame at the stake.

Josh, Emma, and Isaac continue to text, trying to persuade me to go out. Even with Mom's absence, I can't bring myself to leave. It feels too soon to invite them over, especially with the risk of Raj knocking on the door at any time. We haven't heard anything else. The briefing was confidential. He had nothing new to report.

They ask how I am and if I need anything. I don't know what to say. How is it that we can be fluent in a language, in my case two, and still find ourselves at a loss for words? How can we know something so fully and disbelieve it at the same time? Tears come at random times: getting dressed or answering the door or in the shower.

I wish I had the energy to run, but my muscles ache from tension and lack of sleep.

I leave my camera on my desk. If Dad isn't in the picture, I don't want to take it.

Josh's cannonball rock helps, and I roll it in my hands, finding comfort in how things evolve. If a rock's shape is impermanent, certainly our situation must be too.

I can't stop watching the video. Paused, the frame fills with Dad, staring straight at the camera. He looks thinner, and it's hard to see if he's lost any of his slight beer belly. Can't tell. Probably not in a week's time, but the jumpsuit they have him in is baggy. I wonder how many bruises line his skin, if they've punched or kicked him. If he's in pain.

Yes, he's alive, but is he okay? Can he stand? Eat?

He looks tired and scared and anxious. It's a familiar expression. I see it in my own reflection every time I walk down the hall, passing family portraits and framed snapshots. An elaborate portrait gallery filled with Dad's long-dead relatives in Iowa and Mom's extensive family tree in Russia. We have a few photos of Lena up. One of my favorites is of Dad sitting with her on his lap, leaning against his stomach, her face smiling as he reads *Goodnight Moon.*

I'm not sure why they put it on the wall, but there's a photo of Mom and Dad when she's pregnant with me. Mom would have been freshly verbal again having ended her months of silence. They look broken. There isn't any joy in their faces. Not excitement or anticipation—just grief and fear. Dad's face looks the same as it does in the video, in that frozen frame. Desperate and uncertain but doing whatever he needs to survive.

I want to remove the photo from the wall. I don't know if that would bring Mom relief or more pain.

It took a couple of years and fertility treatment for them to have Lena. They nicknamed her Snegurochka, the name of the snow girl from Russia's famous fairytale. Dad used to read the story on New Year's, her celebration day, from an exquisite illustrated book that now sits on my shelf. He'd play Rimsky-Korsakov's opera *The Snow Maiden*. It was his memorial to Lena, and Mom silently endured until she finally confessed she never wanted to hear it again.

In the story, an older man and woman wanted a child. After years of trying unsuccessfully, they magically made a girl from snow. With hands tucked in thin gloves, they molded the snow into the shape of a young girl, forming a head, a slim torso, limbs, hands, and feet. They labored to create perfect ears, fingers, toes, and a nose. When it came to her face, they placed two bright blue beads into the hollow eye sockets, arranged a red ribbon into a smile, and with a twig, added two dimples. After she came to life, she had deep blue eyes, twinkling with beauty, skin as pale as the snow of which she was made, and curly blond hair.

She thrived in winter, enjoying the shivering days and frosty nights. When the seasons changed from bitter cold to mild spring to warm summer days, Snegurochka grew withdrawn and sad. In an attempt to cheer herself up, she joined her friends in the forest for an afternoon of picking wildflowers. As night fell, they built a fire and, holding hands, danced around the flames. One courageous girl leaped over the fire, twirling as she landed. The other girls copied her ballet steps. When Snegurochka's turn came, she jumped over the burning embers and suddenly melted, transformed into a white cloud.

Lena, too, turned into a vapor.

Please, Dad, not you too.

Eighteen

The next morning, Mom finds me in my room, the video playing again on my laptop, muted. I watch Dad's lips move and his hollow eyes. In the middle of the night, I woke and watched the video again, freezing frame after frame, looking for clues to his well-being. I searched for more bruises and cuts and scratches, but even magnified, the film is too grainy to discover much.

One of his fingernails is broken and bloody. I hope nothing else is.

Mom cups my chin and lifts up my face until my eyes meet hers, red-rimmed and distraught. "I don't want you watching that video over and over again. *Ponimayu?*" Understand? "I know you, Charlotte. You obsess. You can't do that with your father. It's not going to bring him home."

"I don't want to go to school," I say. "Everyone will have seen him. I can't face it. Let me stay home another day."

She clucks her tongue, something she used to do when I was little, a sound of disapproval. "Work helps me. School will help you. It was fine to stay home yesterday, but you need to go back. You need to occupy yourself. Why don't you bring Emma home after school?"

She sounds firm but looks pleading. Tatya Nadine is resorting to old techniques to bring Mom back to the living. Yesterday, they moved from the bakery ovens to our kitchen stove, cooking cheese and meat blintzes, light and delicate, precisely the way they have been made for two hundred years. I noticed Mom didn't sample a bite, but she didn't isolate herself in her room until bedtime. She's trying, and she's asking me to do the same.

"Okay," I say. This time, I mean it. I'll go. I won't skip. Mostly because I need to see the Editorial Roundtable and Josh.

"Go shower. I'm sending you to school with pastries."

I can't stop thinking about Uncle Miguel's promise. After Raj called back with nothing new to report, Uncle Miguel swore that the paper was doing whatever it could. He hugged Mom and me at the same time, an arm around each of us, holding on tight. "We're going to get him back," Uncle Miguel had said. "No matter what."

Of course I believe Uncle Miguel more than anything that comes out of Raj's mouth. I have to. I can't imagine otherwise, no matter how I wake up in the middle of the night, a little sweaty and a whole lot scared. I can't let myself think about the fact that Dad might not come home. I keep pushing the thought away, but my fear is stubborn.

As I leave for school, Mom loads me with a box of pastries. We have so much food that I want to walk down Geary Boulevard and distribute it to the homeless and hungry.

I walk into class, and Emma, Isaac, and Josh are busy skimming the newspapers. As soon as they see me, they fold up the pages and place them in a single stack. Megan sweeps them into her desk drawer.

Megan looks at me, her eyes so full of sympathy that I have to look away. I feel my body then, the blood rushing to my fingers and toes, my heart beating as though I had circled Golden Gate Park a hundred times.

I'm torn between Emma and Josh, who moves his chair to make room for me. Emma frowns when I pick Josh, and I immediately feel bad. When I take a seat, he weaves his fingers through mine. He somehow breaks through the rattling feeling I've had since waking up. I drank too much coffee and reached my limit of anxiety. I didn't sleep much again, and when Mom woke me up, I'd just fallen asleep a couple of hours before. She's trying. Hard. Tatya Nadine must be coaching her on an hourly basis: *Leave your room. Talk to your family. Work.* She recited the same lines after they buried Lena.

I place the box of pastries on the table.

"Thank God," Isaac says.

Proud on Mom's behalf, I love that they love her food. They reach for their favorites. Isaac takes two.

If I were to assign them each a pastry, Emma would be *rogaliki,* small baked crescent rolls filled with fruit and cream, everyone's favorite. Isaac would be an almond horn, sweet and straightforward, the popular pastry displayed on the top shelf behind the glass counter. Megan would be *Tulskie prianiki,* gingerbread, the perfect balance of spicy and sweet. Josh would be *sharlotka,* a round sugary cake made with apples, the dessert I crave when I need comfort food.

"I'm not supposed to talk about my dad," I say. "FBI orders."

"Come on, we already know. We're researching like crazy. What are they telling you?" Isaac asks, a little indignant.

Clearly, Raj Singh knows more than he's telling—the question is, how much? I know he's going to keep things from us for many reasons. I'm not an idiot. But what do we do until they decide they can share their information? How long are we supposed to keep this within our apartment when everyone we know will be asking about Dad and what's being done to bring him home?

I look at my friends, who are staring at me, waiting for my answer. Will I do this on my own, or will I let them in?

They're right—they already know.

"Isaac," I say, "have you figured out if the group has a name? The FBI guy said that they're new but some people from other groups are in it. I don't know why there's a new group or anything about them."

Isaac grins. "On it."

Josh leans closer. "I want to show you something," he says.

"You sound like the FBI."

"Come on."

I follow him into the computer closet. Josh turns around a giant monitor so nobody can see the screen from the door. He's wearing the same jacket, the one with the eagle buttons. He takes it off before sitting down, revealing a blue T-shirt with a giant picture of a masked, mustachioed man's face. Josh's arms are irresistible, and all I can think of is being at his house, in his room. I shove my hands into my pockets to stop myself from touching him.

"What's on your shirt?" I ask.

"Guy Fawkes. He's kind of an antiestablishment hero."

I roll my eyes. "Strange choice, don't you think, considering my dad was taken by rebels?"

"Guy Fawkes would have rescued your dad by now." He types faster than anyone I've ever seen, opening several pages in rapid succession.

"Check it out," he says as he presses play.

We watch a video of some family pleading for the release of their son. He plays a couple more. One of the parents of an abducted aid worker in Sudan. Another of a journalist in Syria. Another of a missionary in Colombia.

"Listen," he says, leaning close. "You don't have to be quiet because the FBI tells you to. You know that your dad won't be in the news a week from now." He points to the aid worker's parents. "She's been missing for over a year."

"What do you want me to do?"

"Make a video. Release it now. A video for a video. I'll film you. I can do any editing you need. Whatever you want."

My mind flashes back to the video of Dad, to his bruises.

"I really want to help," he says. "You know we need to keep your dad in the news. Sometimes you have to break some rules to make something good happen."

"Josh, you don't understand. They said that they'll take away our passports. That if we do anything, it's treason."

"They're saying that because they want to control you. They want to do everything their way on their terms. They're not just thinking about bringing your dad home. They're thinking about politics, too."

I straighten my spine, like Mom, and try to conjure the stoicism that she displayed with Raj. *Don't cry. Don't cry. Don't cry.*

Josh stares at me. That never helps. I look at the floor, blinking back tears. He tucks a stray curl behind my ear, and it takes everything I have, every ounce of willpower, to not fall into him.

What would Dad do if Mom went missing? If I did? Everything he possibly could. Rules wouldn't matter. Politics wouldn't matter. Only we'd matter. Family. That's when I make a decision: We'll do whatever we can to bring Dad home.

I take a breath and meet Josh's eyes. "Let me think about it, but maybe. Probably. Just give me a little time, okay?"

Megan steps into the room and puts a hand on my shoulder. "I hate to say this, but we still have a paper to put out. Charlotte, your photos are in, but they want us to make a display of the ones from the winter formal. Can you make prints? I checked and the darkroom is open."

She knows that I wish we were old-school, developing prints weekly rather than producing them digitally. Nothing feels better than being in the darkroom. Except cross-country. Maybe except Josh.

I rummage through my backpack in search of film. At dances and big school events, I always bring both cameras, digital and regular, so I have the option to make prints.

Before heading to the darkroom, I stop to talk to Emma. I can see a flash of hurt in her eyes. It's better if I don't bring it up, especially if there's any hope of her ever accepting Josh, much less liking him. I hug her instead. When I ask her about coming over after school, she says, "Finally."

I pull out two canisters of film, but I'm not sure which one contains the dance photos. I'd forgotten to label them. Guess I'll develop both.

The first roll contains shots from runs and hanging out with the Editorial Roundtable, a week or two before spring break. A lifetime ago. When I rinse a print and hang it to dry, I relive taking the shot. The more I look, the more my other senses surface: the smell of the garden, the taste of the salt-water air, the foggy wind touching my exposed skin. A few weeks ago, I'd taken pictures of the Queen Wilhelmina Tulip Garden in the park. The young tulips blaze in the photos, and the color alone grabs my attention. The stems sway in the breeze and pull the eye along the flowers' curves, the arc of the petals, in an unexpected, almost sensual way. I'm making a life-cycle triptych, hoping to evoke the emotion of birth, full bloom, and the inevitable shedding of petals, of life, only to bloom again the following spring. The three tulip photos were meant to be a gift for Dad's birthday. Now they feel morbid.

I stop myself from examining any more of the pictures, working just hard enough to produce decent prints. Nothing more. I can't think of Dad, not now. I'm barely hanging on right now. If I'm going to make it through a day of school, I have to push my feelings down, swallow them, hide them deep inside my body. It's the only way.

Still, after I finish developing both rolls, I don't leave. I welcome the darkness—a sudden necessity. Things are too real in the light. Too exposed. I wonder how long I can stay in here. I'm sure I have another roll of film in my locker. Maybe two. Megan would probably write me a pass to skip my next class.

Megan knocks. "Safe to come in?"

"Yes," I holler through the door.

She enters and turns on the light and evaluates my photos, including some random shots of students around school. A sly one of Josh. She points to one of Isaac and Emma working together.

"This would be good for the yearbook." She supervises one extracurricular activity, yearbook. I'm the photo editor for that, too.

"Yeah."

In addition to the winter dance pictures of guys in jackets and girls in dresses, the faces of my friends hang in a straight line. Megan fiddles with a shot of Josh standing next to one of the computers. I'd taken it through the doorway, covertly, seduced by his profile. The sun shone through the single window, as small as a jail cell's, illuminating him, but the background looked yellow and orange with a streak of red. I'd caught the light in a strange way, almost overexposed, making him clear but the rest of the photo waves of color.

"He looks like he's in the middle of a lava lamp," Megan says.

"I know," I say. "I totally messed up the lighting. I thought the sun would look good, but the curtain and walls made it look all distorted. Not what I was going for."

She follows the row of pictures and pauses at one of Emma, unclipping it, holding the corners, careful not to smudge.

I walk over to see which one she removed. Emma in Chinatown.

Some weekends, Emma and I play tourist, spending the afternoon blending in with the throngs of visitors. To get to Chinatown, with its lanterns strung high over narrow streets, we boarded a busy bus, clinging to handrails and avoiding the crush of bodies. Emma covered my hand with hers. I remember trying to block out the stench of the man standing next to me. He reeked of a combination of cigarettes, malt liquor, and what I assumed was food rotting in his pockets. I didn't dare look at his face.

Racing cable cars up and down steep hills, we watched the buildings transition from pale colors to a vibrant red. We didn't have an exact destination in mind, since we were there to poke around and people-watch. The squeaking brakes preceded a violent lurch as the bus came to a stop. We ducked under a gaggle of tourists and jumped onto the curb, never so grateful for fresh air. I pointed down the street, and we strolled past the bustling markets to our favorite shop. If you ignored the picked-over souvenirs, you'd find some real gems like wooden clogs, velvet beaded slippers, and slim journals with elegant cloth covers. I'd once bought a Lucky Cat figurine for Mom there to bring good fortune to the kitchen.

Outside, a cluster of parasols hung from the awning. The sun streamed through the fabric and illuminated the patterns of flowers and birds. Camera raised, I took a step back, and the colors filled the frame.

Megan yanks me out of the memory. "You really have a good eye with portraits. You're able to capture the moments of emotion that are more complicated, when someone feels conflicted. Look at Emma. She seems happy, but she's sharing the sidewalk with all of those other people. Her shoulders are hunched. She's trying to take up as little space as possible, but she's giving us that big Emma smile."

Megan puts down the photo and reaches for another. "This one is amazing, Charlotte. Your portraits are haunting, but this is excellent. Much more abstract. You should be very proud of this."

"That was a mistake," I say with a laugh. "I tripped when I took it."

"But look at the angle."

I'd meant to shoot the store's exterior, but instead I shot the sidewalk, captured in a blur, and the scuffed shoes of fellow pedestrians. I take a closer look.

"I think that's bird poop."

Megan smiles. "I don't care what it is. They look like they are walking on a cloud. See?" She runs her finger along the bottom. "You can't tell it's a hard surface. The legs and feet are clear, but the ground isn't. Mistake or not, this is exceptional."

"It wasn't intentional. How can that be exceptional?"

"Experiments and mistakes produce some of the finest work. If I saw this photo anywhere else, I would know you took it. You have a very distinct style. You should show this to Mr. Donoghue. I know you've never taken art with him, but I think he'd appreciate your work and would have some helpful insight about colleges."

She evaluates the rest of my prints, mostly of the winter dance and a few more of Emma, Isaac, and Josh.

"I'm glad you're relying on your friends. No one can go through something like this alone. I know from experience. I saw some terrible stuff when I was in the Peace Corps." Megan winces as she says this. "Trust me."

"You know how you told us at the beginning of the

year that it's never been a more dangerous time to be a journalist?"

Megan nods, but in the dim light, I can barely see her face.

"He may not come home," I say.

She steps closer, and I see her eyes, hesitant and sad. "I'm not going to lie to you. He may not, but he probably will. Most do. Don't give up, and don't forget you're not alone."

She taps one last photo from the dance. A girl and her date wear matching white. The snow queen and king. I remember how they danced like no one else was there. I don't know either of them, just that they're shy and smart and inconspicuous. That night, everyone noticed them; everyone paid attention.

Sometimes the loudest noise comes from a quiet source.

I think of Josh's words: *a video for a video.* I'm not sure if that's the right thing to do, but I know I need to do something. We're not the FBI, but we're not helpless. We have brains and computers and determination. And one another.

Nineteen

Emma fills the house with warmth. She's incapable of silence. She laughs easily, even at the most inappropriate times. Mom remarks that Emma's more like Dad than me, and even though I wish it weren't true, it is.

Even with Emma here, our apartment feels gloomy and freezing. I open all of the curtains and turn up the heat, anything to bring in light and warmth. Ever since Dad was classified as officially missing, I feel like the fog follows me home, permeating the apartment with darkness, thick and cold.

We camp in my room, pulling blankets onto the floor to create a nest. Emma examines the additions to the collaged wall, and I tell her vacation stories. We both marvel at how Mom is a different person with Dad around, evident in the photos. She looks younger and more carefree. Almost happy.

I show Emma my desk drawer full of canisters of film. I'd have to spend three days straight in the darkroom to develop all of them. I explain how I'll bring in a few canisters a week to get them all developed before graduation.

Emma stands and taps a photo I took of my parents in Italy. "Why do you think your dad's gone so much, you know, if it's hard on your mom?"

It's hard on me, too, but I don't say this. It's a selfish thought not meant to be spoken out loud. "Don't know. After I was born, he changed beats and didn't travel. He covered the city council, and Uncle Miguel jokes that he's never seen my dad more miserable. He used to pace during the meetings because he was so bored. He switched back to international stories when I was old enough for preschool."

"I always wondered about that," Emma says.

"My mom calls him restless." I stop and look at Emma. She smiles, waiting for me to continue. It's hard, though, putting this into words. I hear the worry in my voice when I finally speak. "I wonder if he'll want to keep traveling if he comes home. Do you think we can get him to stay?"

Emma returns to the bundle of blankets on the floor and puts both hands on my shoulders. "*When,* Charlotte. Not *if.*"

"Okay," I say, and give her the latest update about Raj Singh's evasive answers to our very direct questions, and then his forceful threat to take away our passports. Emma and I conclude that he's in over his head. A little patronizing. Undoubtedly unqualified.

Emma grabs my laptop and looks him up. "Holy crap, you didn't tell me he's gorgeous. Look at him."

"I've seen him enough, thanks," I say.

Emma laughs. "Well, I haven't."

She pulls up his bio from some conference last year and reads it out loud. Originally from DC, college at Yale, and a master's from Stanford. On one of those resume websites, we confirm that I was absolutely correct: This is his first job out of school. He's been at the FBI for only a year. He's a jock. In his free time, he enjoys travel and skiing. He rows. He plays soccer. On paper, he is worldly and smart. He is young, Megan's age, but inexperienced. He should join his fraternity brothers and do something else, something that doesn't involve hostage negotiations and communicating with major newspapers. Maybe he should go to law school or work on Wall Street. Make some money off that Ivy League education. He should leave the serious work of rescuing my father to the adults.

Emma finds a photo of him at a bar in Palo Alto, where he was crowned the winner of trivia night. Raj, obviously drunk, grins at the camera as a blond girl kisses his cheek.

"Why'd you get a rookie?" she asks. "Doesn't make sense. Everyone pays attention to a missing reporter."

"Yeah, for a couple of days," I say. "Dad won't be in the news next week unless another video is released."

Emma nods and keeps surfing. I want to tell her about my conversation with Josh, but I haven't decided what to do—about the video or anything else. I'm beginning to think it's our best option. Maybe our only one.

"His dad worked for the State Department," Emma says, pointing to a picture of a young Raj with his family. "His mom's a professor at Georgetown. His dad probably got him the job."

"Excellent. Nepotism and no experience. Can't wait to tell Uncle Miguel."

"If anybody is going to find him, it's Miguel. Put a reporter on it—not the government," Emma says.

"You sound like Josh," I say.

Emma slides the computer off her lap and stretches. "You're going to think I'm mean for saying this because you like him so much, and because he's finally decided to pay attention to you, but I don't think you should go out with him."

I roll my eyes. This again.

"He's been suspended twice," she says. "Not detention. *Suspended.* He got arrested once at Critical Mass. I know for a fact that he's barely passing chem. His scores are almost as bad as mine. How is he going to get into college? Did he even apply?"

"God, Emma, you sound like my mom would sound if she were a normal mom."

"You're too good for him. You're going to go to school and become a photojournalist for a big magazine or paper or something. What's he going to be doing—delivering packages on his bike? I don't get why everyone thinks he's so great. I really don't. I know why *you* like him. He's hot. Really hot. And, okay, so his films are kinda cool. It's not like he's a genius, though. You've got to admit that. You deserve someone better. Being hot isn't enough. He'll probably end up in federal prison."

"You're a snob, Emma Archer. And harsh. And wrong. I still love you, but you can't go around calling him an arrogant creep when you're being elitist yourself."

I'm mad. Not super mad, but mad. She can tell, but she pretends she can't. That's Emma. So I'm not surprised when she laughs. "Yes, I am. And I'm your best friend. And he's always been kind of a jerk. Like he's better than us."

I tap her foot with my own. "You don't like him because he's not one of us and he doesn't want to be. And there's nothing wrong with bike messengers."

"Except they get hit by cars and don't look like they shower regularly. All I'm saying is we're about to find out where we're going to school, and now's the time to care about our futures."

Over the last few years, I've itemized Josh's many, many good qualities. I'm not the only girl in school who likes him—I pay close attention in the cafeteria. If I haven't convinced Emma by now, I doubt I can. She knew I liked Josh when she suggested I go out with Kyle, who was a distraction, someone meant to make me forget about Josh. Not that it worked.

"Josh is getting an A in English," I say, and leave it that. I'm not going to debate Emma. She's relentless and caffeinated. I won't win, and it doesn't matter. It's not like she's going to change my mind about him.

She wraps her arms around me and squeezes tight. Sometimes she feels more like family than anyone else.

After a few quiet moments, Emma says, "I'm worried about colleges. Really worried. My math and science grades are totally mediocre, and my SAT scores are crap. I don't want to go someplace without you, but how the hell am I going to get into Berkeley and NYU? I'll be lucky if I get into my backup schools."

It seems inconceivable for Emma not to get in. She earns practically perfect grades in English, history, and any class that requires writing papers. She does more extracurriculars than anyone else. Her family even volunteers on Thanksgiving, serving meals to the homeless. And, unlike mine, her family can afford to send her wherever she wants to go. Grad school, too.

"I don't think you need to worry. We're just stuck in this in-between place," I say. "It's going to be torture until we know what's next."

"I'm worried about you, too," she says. "Your entire life is in-between right now."

"I know," I say, closing my eyes a second to contain my tears. "I think things might be changing with my mom, though. She's talking to me more. That's good."

Emma says, "That's really good. I found a book on my mom's desk called *Supporting Your Child's Destiny: Nurturing Growth While Letting Go.* I read most of it last weekend."

"What life lessons did you learn?"

"She highlighted about half the book. Random stuff. But she wrote notes in the margins, and they're all about me. This book was filled with questions: Is your child a risk taker? An introvert? What motivates your child? Stuff like that."

"What'd she write?"

"She circled things on the lists, like most of the outgoing traits and then half of the introverted traits with notes about how I couldn't be boxed into just one category. The weird thing was how much she got right."

"Are you going to tell her that you looked at it?" I ask.

"No. She's talking like the book now, though. She's asking

me more questions about what I want, and she's being supportive. She said that we all end up at the right place even if it doesn't seem so at the beginning."

We rest quietly for a while, and I assume Emma's mind is just as full as mine with the images of near and distant cities and how, even alone, we would navigate them.

I don't allow myself to think of a future without Dad. He'll come home, and as a family, we'll drive to my new school, the car filled with boxes. He'll haul them up the stairs into my dorm room, which I'll share with Emma. We'll unpack and decorate. Whenever I call home, Dad will be the one who answers. Eventually, his voice will sound common again, something I love but take for granted. The voice of someone who is always there.

Emma hugs me again. "We'll be okay. My mom and her book say so."

"That's good enough for me."

It will have to be.

Twenty

It takes five steps to develop a photograph in the darkroom. Four of those steps require darkness. Sometimes when I wash the print, the last step, I leave the lights off, using my hands instead of my eyes, feeling my way through the dark.

I slept only a couple of hours last night. And then only in the nest I'd made with Emma. After another dream about Dad covered in bruises, I crawled out of bed onto the floor, wrapping myself up in the pile of blankets. I woke up with the image of Dad in the video more vivid in my mind than those now emerging on the photo paper. I rinse and hang, rinse and hang.

I need to develop those rolls of film, and given how the darkroom is one of the few places where I feel calm, I decided to come in early today to start.

Now I wish I hadn't.

When Tatya Nadine moved out of the flat upstairs and into her Pacifica condo, she left a horde of old furniture in the basement, desks and headboards, and boxes of books. She granted me permission to take a vanity table and chair into the backyard, where, bored during summer break when Dad was on some trip and Mom in one of her quiet spells, I decided to take a self-portrait. Well, really a portrait with Lena. Nothing's more morbid than taking a picture of photos of your now-dead sister.

I sat in the chair facing what was supposed to be my reflection. Instead, I'd scanned and blown up a picture of Lena, one where she most resembled me. Russians believe the soul leaves the body and enters the mirror, creating a reflection. I wanted to capture my connection to Lena, how our souls are intertwined and how I couldn't look at my reflection without seeing her. Or, really, how I believe that Mom probably wishes I were Lena. That Lena had lived. That she never had to have me, her replacement who nearly killed her.

It took hours to get the right perspective, but when I did, even I couldn't believe the effect. It had been a typical foggy summer morning, and I'd shot it in black and white. Now that I see the print, it truly looks like the picture of Lena is my own reflection.

I'd been so out of it this morning that I forgot to tell

Megan I was here. So when she opens the door, she startles when she sees me. At least the lights are on.

"Another early morning, Charlotte?"

"Yeah, sorry. I should have asked."

"No." She shakes her head and smiles. "You never have to get permission to use the darkroom—as long as it's free."

Curiosity gets the better of her, and she unclips a print. "These are different. I've never seen you do a self-portrait."

"I was just playing around. I didn't mean to show them to anyone."

"I'm glad you did," she says. "Are you finished in here?"

"Yeah, for now. They need to dry."

Megan returns the picture. "Come into the classroom. Coffee's brewing."

Newspapers rest atop each table. I wonder if we're back to our usual seat assignments, no longer clustered together strategizing about digging up information on Dad and Ukraine. I hope not. I want to stay huddled together, with Megan taking charge of our investigative work. I want to start off the morning with the Editorial Roundtable reporting any new discoveries before going about our usual duties with the whole staff during first period. Editing copy. Designing the pages. Writing photo captions.

Megan fills two mugs, adds milk to both, and brings a few sugar packets to the table. She knows I take my coffee candy-sweet. A magazine, one of her favorites published by a nonprofit committed to in-depth reporting, rests on the table. I love their photo essays. It's open to a page with a single shot of a man's face, maybe his passport photo, accompanied by a letter:

Dear Mr. President,

William Baxter published with National Public Radio, the *Boston Globe, Chicago Tribune,* and *Denver Post.* He graduated from Columbia University's journalism school with one goal in mind: show the world the devastating impact of war. When the conflict in Ukraine intensified in 2013, Will booked a flight to report the news.

The day before his twenty-seventh birthday, he traveled to Kharkiv to cover a bombing. We know he was taken hostage, and we believe—we must believe—he is still alive.

Mr. President, you have been a vocal proponent of a free press and how essential it is in times of war and strife. Reporters Without Borders just released their latest report, and more journalists were harmed and murdered last year than ever before.

I am writing to ask you to use your full power and diplomacy to bring William Baxter home.

Will traveled to Ukraine, as he had to Syria and Sudan, to show the world the reality, horror, and truth about war. The human cost. He risked his life to tell these stories. As a country, we owe it to him to do everything within our power to secure his return.

Sincerely,

Sign and share the petition at www.BringWillBaxterHome.org

"He was taken years ago," I say. In that amount of time, I will have graduated from high school and be almost done with college—while Dad rots in some horrible dark room, covered in bruises and completely forgotten by everyone but me and Mom and Tatya Nadine and Uncle Miguel. My stomach clenches, and I push the coffee away.

"Reporters have been kept for years by governments like

North Korea and Iran, but this is different. Your dad and Will Baxter were taken by rebels. There's no one to negotiate with in that case. Rebels don't have an ambassador, and the U.S. law is clear: It's treason to try to negotiate with terrorists. So Will Baxter's family is going public to put the pressure on the government."

"And to try to keep him in the news before it's a lost cause," I say.

"Exactly." Megan sips her coffee, leaving a smudge of red lipstick on the rim. "I wanted to show you this. A lot of people are going to tell you what to do, Charlotte. Do what feels right and honest. Just because someone has power doesn't mean they're correct."

"You sound just like my dad," I say. "He's the only person I could really talk to in situations like this. You know, if I'm feeling overwhelmed. But he's the reason I'm feeling this way and, obviously, he's not here."

Megan smiles, and I'm so grateful that Mr. McGuire retired and I hope he's enjoying his days on the golf course. "You know where to find me," she says. "And we'll have Isaac research Will Baxter. He's done with his water conservation story. He is accusing the swim team of creating drought conditions."

"Of course he is," I say.

"One more thing, Charlotte. Those photos of yours, and

the more recent portraits. They're really good. You know how valuable you are to the paper, but I want you to think about other forms of photography. Less journalistic. I think that's where your heart is. Less like your dad and more like you."

She means to be encouraging. Complimentary. Kind. I should be gracious and grateful. I shouldn't feel like I do, with my hands squeezed into fists and tears in my eyes. She's right—that's what I want. But with Dad gone, I can't do anything besides photojournalism. I want to be like Dad. I *need* to be like him. He's strong and smart and has a lightness that lifts up everyone around him. If I'm not like him, then I'm like Mom, fragile and afraid.

"Oh, Charlotte," Megan gasps, seeing the look on my face. "I didn't mean for you to think that you aren't good at the paper. You're very talented." She touches my hand. "That's my point. I want you to be open to all kinds of photography. Don't limit yourself."

I nod and wipe my nose with the back of my hand. "Okay."

"I want to show the prints, the ones that are drying in the darkroom, to Mr. Donoghue."

Mr. Donoghue resembles a sock puppet or Muppet, with oversized features and a smile that fills half his face. His students adore him.

"It's just that I feel closer to my dad when I'm working on the paper. He's the news, if that makes sense. When we talk about stories and edits and captions and everything, I can hear him say the words. And I need to spend these two hours a day here with you guys. I don't want to give that up. Especially now."

"I'm not suggesting you do. But you have something in your photos, the newer ones in particular. It's special. It's not like you have to choose one kind of photography. The whole point is to learn and explore and grow. That might be good for you right now."

I've always wanted to travel, knowing from an early age, thanks to Mom's immigration and Dad's job, that there's a huge world to explore. Now, though, I want everything so small that it will fit into one place, one house, even one room. I want containment and safety, with everyone I love together.

Outside of my family—in the apartment and bakery— this classroom and the darkroom are just that.

I wonder how Will Baxter's family has survived the waiting and grief. Letters and phone calls and petitions can go only so far. The public needs to know what's going on. Will disappeared in every way—abducted and then forgotten by everyone but those who know him. I refuse to let that happen to Dad.

Twenty-One

Will Baxter has been missing for years, and no one knows his name—until today, not even news nerds like us.

I trust Josh.

I trust Uncle Miguel.

Raj Singh is secretive and useless.

Mom keeps getting up in the middle of the night to call her cousin in Russia. She's ignoring the FBI's instructions, placing her faith in family.

Isaac is the one who's been scouring the news looking for information on the rebels, discovering the news stories about the village bombings and a downed plane.

A video for a video.

Josh and I sit in the computer closet while Megan referees an argument between Isaac and Emma over which story should go on the next edition's front page. A weekly occurrence. Emma usually wins.

"Okay," I say, looking at Josh, "let's do it. But I want to figure out when to release it. And how. I want to talk to Uncle Miguel because the *Tribune* should have first dibs."

"Really?" he asks. "'Cause I think it's a brilliant idea, and I'm not just saying that because it's mine."

"It's a good one," I say.

"This is going to bring him home." His face is full of hope. His mouth curves into a smile, and this time, I don't hold back because we're at school. I trace his lips with my finger, and for the briefest moment, when he kisses me, he makes me forget everything.

Twenty-Two

Uncle Miguel has started dropping by, sometimes in the afternoon, other times for dinner. He gives us updates. Usually there's nothing new. Sometimes general news about the current state of things in Ukraine: cleaning up the villages, updated numbers of the missing, and then meetings with the publisher. He tells us everything.

But tonight at dinner, I'm the one with something to report.

I give them details about the now-almost-completely-forgotten Will Baxter and his years of confinement. We talk about our fear that the same thing will happen to Dad, who, while crafty and charming, can be surly and rebellious. Not a good combination when dealing with rebels. Hence the many bruises. He's a man who will always fight back, especially if people are at risk of getting harmed. Dad is all about helping the underdog.

"I don't want to sit around and wait for the FBI," I say. "We still don't know anything, and France got Pascal back. This is ridiculous."

"It is," Uncle Miguel says. "We need to be careful, though. The FBI is working closely with the paper, but I don't think we can lose this opportunity to keep Jeremiah in the news. He'll fade quickly. The window is small. Question is, what do we do with it?"

Mom leans forward. "What if I talked? You could interview me."

"Yeah," I agree. "It could be an exclusive with the *Tribune*. Dad's on your staff after all. You should be able to run something, right?"

Uncle Miguel looks at the two of us. "It's a good idea." He sips his beer. "The thing is, I can't run anything about Jeremiah without approval, and there's no way the publisher will print something without the FBI knowing."

My phone beeps. A text from Emma. "What if we didn't run it in the *Tribune*?" I ask. "What if the school paper did it?"

Uncle Miguel smiles at me. "It won't reach enough people."

"Not on its own," I say, looking at each of them. "But we could post it online and on social media. Then the *Tribune* could write a story about the post, right? You could even be the one to write it so it's handled right."

Uncle Miguel polishes off his beer and stares at the can, turning it in his hand like the list of ingredients contains vital information. "It's not a bad idea, but let's hold off. I want to see how things are at the paper. Let me float the exclusive interview idea."

I can't hide my exasperation. "We don't have time. That's the point! We can't sit back and let what happened to Will Baxter happen to Dad."

It takes everything—absolutely everything—to not tell them about the idea of doing the video. I want them to know that we can do this—all of us—if we work together. We each have things we can do: Mom and Tatya are in touch with family. Uncle Miguel knows absolutely everyone working in the media and can leverage the *Tribune*. The Editorial Roundtable will make the video. I just need to know if Uncle Miguel will run it.

Mom leans close to me, all gentle, and tells me it's okay. "We're not going to wait long. Just let Miguel talk to the people at the paper."

"That's right, Lottie," he says. "I'm talking about hours, not days, okay?"

"You'll let me know what they say?" I ask.

"Yep. As soon as I have the conversation. Maybe the publisher is still in the office. I'll head in now—try to get us an answer tonight."

When he stands, we join him, forming a makeshift circle. I think of football players huddled at the start of the game, feeding off one another's energy and optimism and anxiety.

If we were other people, another family, we'd collapse into a group hug or high fives or some display of comradery or affection.

Uncle Miguel kisses my cheek. Soon after he leaves, Mom starts heading down to the bakery to finish cleaning up after the day's work and prep for the morning.

I pick up my phone and text Josh, asking if he's ready to do this thing. Making the video is the right choice. I ask if he can meet me at the café for coffee tomorrow morning. He doesn't make me wait. Yes, he replies. He'll be there at eight. My heart skips a little. It's not only about the video; I want to be near him, just for a while, to make me feel better. To feel something besides this strung-out, rattling desperation that fills me all the time now.

Next, Emma and Isaac.

Blue Danube 8:00 a.m. tomorrow? Bringing Josh. Be nice.

They both text back immediately. They're in, and promise to behave.

I'm not sure how my friends will be with Josh outside of school. Emma and Isaac probably aren't surprised that I invited Josh, but maybe that he agreed to come. They'll probably scowl. Isaac might be sarcastic. Emma will probably be painfully polite. I can't worry about that right now. They'll have to deal. For this, I'll need all of them.

My phone beeps again with a text to me and Mom from Uncle Miguel.

No definitive answer from publisher yet. He's calling a conference with the board and will let me know their decision sometime tomorrow.

No definitive answer. All the more reason to make the video.

In times of stress and trauma, people form bonds, some temporary, some permanent. Maybe this whole situation with Dad will finally bond Josh and Emma and Isaac. Granted, it's my trauma, not theirs. But still.

On Saturday morning, I'm dressed and ready long before I need to head to the café, full of nervous energy. When it's finally time, I pop into the bakery on my way out to tell Mom where I'm going. She and Tatya seem relieved that I'm spending time with friends this weekend instead of staying cooped up in the apartment.

When I get to the Blue Danube, I see Josh's bike chained out front. He's sitting in a far corner, laptop open, drinking an enormous cup of coffee. A skullcap hides his dark hair, making his eyes appear even bigger, especially when he looks at me. I'm still getting used to this version of Josh, who texts me all the time, who skips school with me, who is determined to help bring my father home. Before, he was like an elusive animal in a nature documentary, the kind photographers pursue to get that one picture. At school, I'd scan the halls and classrooms and cafeteria for a glimpse of him in his native habitat. Now, he's tame. No longer skittish.

I rest my bag on the table. He stands, all gentlemanly. When they took Dad, I kept thinking, *This can't be real.*

With Josh, when his lips meet mine, I think, *This really is happening.*

Why do terrible and wonderful things occur at the same time? The terrible eclipses the wonderful—no matter what. Is it the only way we can stay grateful, to know that with gain comes loss? That, no matter what, happiness can never be a permanent state of being?

Emma and Isaac walk in. "I'm going to get coffee," I tell Josh.

As soon as I'm close enough, Em nudges me with her elbow. "Are we all here to get to know him better, or do you have news?"

"It would be nice if you got along, but there's a bigger purpose. Not news. A plan. We need to do something," I say.

"Then we should," Isaac says.

I fill them in on the conversation with Uncle Miguel and how we're still waiting on a verdict from the *Tribune*. If they won't run a story, then we're stuck.

Isaac orders a triple espresso, and Emma keeps it calm with a chai. I hope she balances him out.

"Let's go hang out with your boyfriend," Isaac says.

"Don't be a dickwit," Emma says. "You promised."

"And don't call him my boyfriend. He's Josh. He's not anyone new. Isaac, you guys went to the same middle school."

"Exactly," Isaac says. "I know what I'm talking about."

I know he's kidding, but I'm not exactly in a joking mood. "Stop. Please. Not today. Just behave. Pretend we're in class, if that helps. Pretend Megan is forcing you to be nice."

Isaac smiles dreamily at the mention of Megan, and lust lulls him into silence.

They exchange hellos with Josh, who returns them with equal formality. I feel like I'm having tea at Buckingham Palace, with all the forced niceties. I just want them to be as normal with one another as they are with me. I add a sugar packet to my latte and stir. "Josh, do you want to explain the plan?" I ask.

Emma and Isaac listen without interrupting.

"That's good," Isaac says. "Do what the rebels are doing—make a video. Everyone will see it."

"Yeah, but what will be in the video?" Emma asks.

"Just Charlotte," Josh says. "We'll make two, one in English and one in Russian."

"That's kind of genius," Emma says.

Josh gives me a smile and says, "Anyone would listen to you."

Isaac almost knocks over all of our cups as he rummages through his backpack. He flips to a blank page in his spiral notebook. "I'll start on the script now. The American one should be straightforward. Bring him home, right? The Will Baxter pitch. What about the Russian one?"

"Set him free. That you want to negotiate," Josh says.

"We can't say that. The FBI was super clear—it's treason. We're not allowed." I look at each of them to drive the point home. "We can ask them to set him free. Tell them that he's a journalist and he can write about their demands and everyone will listen."

"Except there's no way in hell your dad will," Emma says. "He's not going to go from being their hostage to being their spokesperson. Your dad would never, ever do that. Not a single decent journalist would."

She's right. Dad wouldn't say anything that he didn't mean, not for his captors. These are people who bomb villages. He won't do anything to help them. He'd sacrifice himself first.

"Just tell them to release your dad," Isaac says. "The

point is to get news coverage. Let's get all over Ukraine and Russia too. That should get people's attention."

"How much trouble is this going to get us in?" Emma asks. I know she's thinking about the college letters that will be in the mail any day now.

"Does it matter?" Josh asks.

"Some of us have plans for after graduation. You know, college. I want to help, but I don't want to get arrested. Not everyone wants to get suspended like you."

Josh opens his mouth to speak, looks at me, and closes it again. He shakes his head. "You're an editor," he says, looking right at Emma. "You know how important it is to get all the facts before reaching a conclusion. Maybe you should apply that to me. You don't know what happened."

"Tell us, then," Isaac says.

"It's not my story to tell. We're here to help Charlotte, so maybe save the righteous judgment for another day." Josh sounds like he's delivered this speech before. I wonder how many times and in what situations.

I catch Emma rolling her eyes, and I shoot her a quasi-glare, enough of a stink eye to get her to remember her promise. *Be nice.*

"Okay," she says. "But I want to hear more later."

"There's nothing else to tell," Josh says, clearly annoyed. "Where should we film the video?"

"Emma's house," I say. "My mom always says it looks Sovietesque with all the concrete. That okay?"

"Yeah. My parents are away for the weekend—that's why I'm still on my takeout and Pop-Tart diet."

"Okay, I'll finish the U.S. script," Isaac says. "Want to take a crack at the Russian one, Josh?"

An olive branch. Thank you, Isaac.

"I don't think Charlotte needs a script to talk about her dad," Josh says. "But thanks for asking. Really." .

Isaac nods. When Isaac is quiet, things are fine. He's quick to speak up and quick to get offended, so you always know where you stand with him.

"Let's bring Jeremiah Lang home," Isaac says, raising his coffee cup.

"And to hell with the FBI," Emma says.

"We agree on that," Josh says.

We toast to my father's safe return. To doing something on our own. Emma, Isaac, and Josh may never be friends, but at least they're here with me.

Twenty-Three

We drive to Emma's house together, leaving Josh's bike chained in front of the café. He seems reluctant to give it up, even temporarily. I think he's the type of person who always has an exit strategy.

Roller coasters fill me with unquantifiable horror, but they pale in comparison to riding shotgun with Emma. I hang my head out the window like a joyriding dog, welcoming the fresh air. When Josh suggests she slow down, Emma laughs in response. We snake through winding streets bearing the names of the planets. She lives on Jupiter.

We all climb out of the car, knees weak from the drive. I wait for Josh, who looks a little green.

"You'll get used to her driving," I say.

"Have you?"

I shrug. "Sort of."

"My favorite spot in the city," Josh says, pointing to Sutro

Tower, the giant candy-striped TV tower atop Twin Peaks. "That's my production company's name. Sutro Films."

"You have a production company?" I ask.

"Yeah, I had to create one when I entered that film festival. It's just me and my brother."

The tower, with its three giant prongs, is visible from many angles in the city. "I've never been up there." I pull out my camera, and take a shot of the tower, the top rising into the low, thick clouds.

"You have to go sometime. It's beautiful at night. You can see most of the city. The bridges and the bay. I'll take you."

I wrap my cardigan tighter around me. The fog rolled in and never left. "Let's go inside."

When I first saw Emma's house, it took a while to adjust. They don't have many things, but everything they do have is exquisite. The entire house, except for Emma's and her brother's rooms, looks ready for a magazine shoot, *Architectural Digest* or *Dwell*. Not staged, exactly. Curated. The house, along with all that fills it, is a work of art.

Dad believes buying art is a waste of money. Instead, buy a plane ticket and visit museums and monuments. See art in context. It's an experience, not a commodity. Still, the few times he's picked me up at Emma's, the admiration was plain on his face.

"Over here," Emma says as she moves a table and chair away from the wall. "Stand away from the table."

Josh checks the shot on his phone. "Move to the left. There. Stop. Good."

In the car, Josh convinced everyone that I'd sound forced if I read from a script. I don't want to look like a hostage myself, he insisted. I need to be natural. I need people to pay attention.

"Just be yourself," Josh says.

What does that even mean? I glance at Josh, Emma, and Isaac. They all, more or less, know who they are and what they want. I have a general sense, but nothing fully formed. Not yet, anyway. Not since Dad left. Not since Megan suggested I approach photography more like art. The thing is, I know she's right.

"Okay, look at me," Josh says. "Ready?"

"Wait!" Emma hollers. I try to see what's wrong. "Makeup. You need makeup."

"No, she doesn't," Josh says.

Emma never leaves the house without putting on mascara and lipstick. I'm the opposite.

"Oh yes, she does." Emma makes a swatting motion with her hand, a dismissive gesture, barely kinder than the middle finger. She squints at me. "Pucker," she says. We've done this millions of times. Before school pictures and parties and dances. She's a perfectionist with the most random things, and makeup is one. If only she applied this level of concentration to chemistry.

She smooths my curls. "There. Better. Now you're all set," she says.

It's Josh's turn to roll his eyes. "Okay," he says. "Charlotte, start whenever you're ready. Look and talk directly to the phone."

I stumble when I say my name. It takes four times. I'm a toddler trying to speak in complete sentences. My name. Dad's name. He's missing. We want him home safe. With each take, I get out a few more sentences, but it's clumsy and hardly newsworthy.

I want to scream. I wish I could do a photo montage instead. Here, look at my brilliant and kind father. Here is my fragile mother who will die a spiritual death if he doesn't come home soon. Look at me. I need him home or I'll be almost orphaned, living with a ghost. Two, if you count Lena, who Mom keeps alive with her palpable grief.

"Just be yourself," Josh says again.

"I need a break," I say, and go hide in the bathroom.

Even the bathtub is beautiful.

I look at the mirror and pretend I'm looking at Dad. Come home. I'm flustered and frustrated and wish Raj Singh and the FBI would do their damn job so I didn't have to do this damn video.

It's easier and harder having Josh here.

I don't want to do this, but it has to be me. Mom is the only other one, and there's no way she'd support our rogue campaign, no matter how upset she is with the FBI.

Emma comes in without knocking. It is her house. "Do you want me to hold up signs? Maybe a script is a good idea after all."

"No, that isn't it." I turn to face her. "I'm not good in front of the camera. I wish I could film you. Or Isaac. Even Josh, but he would kind of suck at this."

"Yes, worse than you." She smiles and pokes my arm. "You're not bad at speaking. You're just thinking too much. What if I stand next to Josh and you talk to me?"

"We can try it," I say.

"Talk about Will Baxter. Say how long he's been gone and how the government has to do something. Enough is enough. Talk to the camera—to me—just like you explained everything at the café. You can do this."

I pretend I'm about to race, that I've stretched and am ready to run the distance. I take a deep breath. "Okay, let's try again."

When I'm in place, Josh asks Isaac to move to the other side. His shadow is ruining the shot. Emma stands next to Josh, and when she nods, I begin. My name is Charlotte Lang. My father, Jeremiah Lang, is a reporter for the *San*

Francisco Tribune. Last week he was kidnapped by rebels in Ukraine. When I mention Will Baxter and the years since his abduction, my voice wavers. I notice Emma notice. I squeeze my hands into fists and dig my nails into my palms. I want to look at Josh, for just a second, but I need to have a steady gaze. *Look at Emma. Don't cry.* I take another breath, deeper than normal, but hopefully not too obvious.

France protected Pascal Baudin. They paid the ransom and brought him home. The United States needs to do everything in their power to bring home my father and Will Baxter. I quote Megan about how a free press is essential to democracy. Are we really going to abandon those who seek to tell the truth? Are they going to leave my dad there to be abused and maybe tortured and killed? My voice breaks.

Every American should care about my father. The government should use diplomacy and force and all available resources to bring him home. If they won't pay the ransom, then they need to figure out how to bring him, Will Baxter, and all kidnapped journalists home. My father is the bravest man on the planet. He leaves his family behind to tell the stories about the families ripped apart by earthquakes and fires and hurricanes. He thinks the world needs to see the truth, the suffering, so we remember that we're all connected. We're vulnerable and fragile and precious. That was what my father was doing when he was taken. He deserves to come home. He's not done telling stories. He's not done helping people. I need him. My mother needs him. He needs to come home.

"That's it," I say. Tears stream down my cheeks, and I suspect my mascara resembles Mom's raccoon eyeliner.

No one speaks. Josh stares at his phone, and Emma and Isaac stare at me. "Sorry," I say. I blew it. Again. I'm about to retreat to the beautiful bathroom, but Emma stops me.

"That was incredible." She steps forward, and I see that she's crying too. "You were perfect."

Isaac nods. "You're going to break the Internet."

I look at Josh. "See," he says. "I told you to be yourself. Think you can do the same thing in Russian?"

"Maybe in a minute," I say, my voice a little shaky. "I don't want to cry again."

"Not to take my director role too seriously, but I think you should do it now," Josh says, the phone still in his hand. "Don't think too much. Remember, this time, you're talking to the guys who took your dad. It's okay to get emotional."

"He's right," Emma says.

Isaac walks over to Emma, taking the place next to her. We're all in this together.

I want to sit or at least have a drink of water, but they're right, get it over with. Something shifts. Tears dry. Eyes clear. My hands return to fists, but now it isn't because I might cry.

I'm too angry. I assume Mom's ballet posture, her straight spine. Josh nods and I begin, although now there's nothing soft-spoken about me. I don't stare at Emma; I stare right at the phone. I don't know what the rebels look like, just the hand of the guy who pointed a gun at my father. I tell them that Dad is a good man and he came to help. They kidnapped someone who cares about the Ukrainian and Russian people. He has family ties to Russia, and they are harming someone who respects the culture. They should do the right thing and release him.

Once again, I finish and am met with stares.

"It's like you were a completely different person," Isaac says. "I've never seen you like that. I couldn't understand a word you said, but wow. Wow."

"I pretended you were one of them," I say. "That helped."

"You were a little scary," Emma says. "In a good way."

I couldn't recite my exact words, but I have a sense of how I looked and sounded. Like Mom before her layer cake of losses.

My phone beeps. A text from Uncle Miguel.

No go on story.

"Oh no," I say as I hold up my phone for them to read.

"It's up to us, then," Josh says. He turns to Isaac, and they start talking about when and where to post the video.

"I think we should blanket it," Josh says. "Total

saturation. Post all over social media and the news sites."

"Maybe we start with the news and see where it goes. We probably don't have to do more work than that," Isaac says.

"Let me talk to Uncle Miguel and my mom first," I say. "I don't want to do this without checking with them since the paper can't run anything."

"Will they stop us?" Josh asks.

"Maybe," I say. "But I need to ask them. Uncle Miguel can help us decide where to send it. Maybe we give it to CNN as an exclusive or something. Probably should be broadcast. He'll know what's best. I'll let you know ASAP."

"Let's watch it," Emma says, and the three of them gather around Josh's phone.

I never like looking at myself, and I really don't have a desire to see myself cry. I watch them watch me. They take turns smiling and nodding, obviously happy with how it turned out. I wonder how Dad felt when they filmed the video of him, when he stared into the camera and recited the rebels' script.

After a few seconds, I ask them to turn it off. We don't need to see the whole thing. I feel disembodied, like the girl on the screen isn't me. Isn't real.

Twenty-Four

I've spoken all of my words to the camera.

I'm quiet as we move back the furniture and quiet on the drive home. Emma and Isaac and Josh are giddy and optimistic. They aren't convinced the video will spur the rebels to free Dad, but they know how news spreads, how it takes over a conversation.

All I can think about is Dad, the marks on his face, the way he looked at the camera. And Will Baxter. His family circulates petitions. They've been waiting in this limbo hell for years. Will I graduate from high school, then college, and still have Dad hidden as a hostage in Ukraine? How are we supposed to carry on with our lives when he's there, captive? How do the Baxters get through the day?

Josh and Isaac banter about how to best pressure the government. Emma drops Isaac off first, then Josh at the café so he can reclaim his bike. I promise to keep them posted. I'll text after I talk to Mom and Uncle Miguel. We'll make a plan. We'll see each other tomorrow.

Emma wants to come up, but I'm too tired. She says she understands. She looks disappointed, though. We're used to sharing everything. But only Mom can share this.

She's in the living room, resting on the couch with her eyes closed. She sits up when I come in. She smiles, but her eyes are red. "Look what came in the mail."

A stack of letters, some in thick envelopes and others in thin. My future is spelled out in that stack of paper. I always imagined we'd open them together, the three of us, Mom, Dad, and me. I want to be excited, but more than anything, I miss him beyond belief. I wipe the tears from my cheeks.

"I know," Mom says. "He should be here. Just know that he's proud of you. Me too."

I take the seat next to her, and she wraps her arms around me. "It's going to be okay," she says.

More than anything, I want to believe her, but I can't, not entirely. I open the slim one first, a rejection from Brown University. I feel both crushed and relieved. I drop the letter and rest my head on Mom's shoulder, not caring if she's feeling maternal or not. We both cry, for Dad and for our lost future. Nothing feels important, not with him gone.

She wipes her nose. "That's the one in Rhode Island?" she asks.

"Yeah. Emma really wanted to go there. It's a good school, but I mostly applied to be with her."

She hugs me tight, harder than she has in years, maybe more than she ever has.

"You need to be strong, Charlotte. No matter what happens. Be stronger than me. Before you open another letter, promise you won't do what I did. Break. Stop living. Promise you'll go to school."

This only makes me cry harder. "I can't promise anything right now. Don't make me. Please."

Mom does something I've needed for so long, for my entire life: she holds me. She doesn't say anything. She just tightens her arms and lets me cry. I'm not sure how long we stay like that, but I feel myself calm down with every breath. Her arms are boa-constrictor-tight, and I suddenly feel like it's going to be okay—no matter what. She's here. She may disappear a little, but she's never gone completely. We have each other and Uncle Miguel and Tatya Nadine.

I squeeze her back before pulling away. "Let's see who wants me."

Mom hands me a thick envelope, the telltale sign of an acceptance. She laughs when I see the return address: New York University.

"Right now, your dad is smiling," she says. "I bet he has a sixth sense that you got in."

"Do you still want me to go away?"

She shakes her head. "I never wanted you to go away, *moya lyubov'.*" My love. "I want you to have adventures. I want you to live. That doesn't mean I don't want you. Understand?"

I'm tempted to press, to ask her if she really means it, if she can promise that if Dad never comes home, she'll be here, present, awake. Not in that strange sleepwalking state she can inhabit for days. But we're both strung out, and I can't take a single other hard thing. Not one.

Two more college rejections: Northwestern and the University of Southern California. Not my top choices.

We create two stacks, the three rejections and then the acceptances: NYU, Emerson, Berkeley, and San Francisco State. So my choices are New York City, Boston, the East Bay, or running and biking distance from home.

She hugs me again. "Your dad would be very proud of you. I am too. Sick of Chinese food yet? I don't have anything for dinner, and I know you're tired of pastries. Mu shu?"

"Potstickers, too."

I re-read the acceptance letters as Mom calls the restaurant. She's ordering too much food. We'll live off leftovers.

A few hours later, Mom and I curl up on the couch and watch another sci-fi movie, one that didn't tempt us when in the theaters. I polish off the last of the pot stickers, now cold. A text came in from Emma a while ago, but I want to be with Mom. Emma probably came home to her college letters too. Suddenly, someone knocks on the door, fast and determined. When Mom answers, Raj Singh comes in. He's furious. Shaking mad.

"Do you have any idea what you've done?" he shouts. He stares at me, his eyes disapproving. He looks at Mom. "Has she told you? Change the channel—it's all over the news."

I bolt upright. My stomach clenches. I practically double over. I feel like someone has crushed my middle. I reach for my phone and read Emma's text.

He posted it. CALL ME!!!!!

It's not Dad on the TV screen this time, or Pascal. It's me, with tears running down my cheeks. Mom's eyes volley between me and the TV, confused. I see her hands shake as she works the remote. My face is everywhere. When she turns to meet my eyes, it's like I'm the terrorist. I never thought she'd look at me so furiously, with so much anger and blame. I stare at the floor.

Uncle Miguel doesn't knock. He rushes past Raj without a word and stands in front of the TV. "Lottie, what the hell were you thinking?"

"I didn't do it!"

Raj folds his arms across his chest. "You're on television

saying your government is failing to bring your father home. What exactly didn't you do?"

"I made the video, but no one was supposed to do anything until I talked to you, Uncle Miguel. I thought you would know what we could do with it."

Raj's phone rings. He declines the call and continues to perfect his angry stare. "You were supposed to be discreet. You were supposed to let the FBI handle this. Did you really think this would help? These people aren't reasonable. They're not going to release Jeremiah because a kid makes a video. They'll probably retaliate in some way. They may beat him, or worse."

"That's enough," Uncle Miguel says in the most forceful tone I've ever heard him use.

I look at Raj and Uncle Miguel. Retaliate by beating Dad? They'd do that because of me? It was supposed to be in the news to help Dad, not hurt him. I swallow hard and try to breathe. What have I done?

"Miguel, please move," Mom says in her scary quiet voice. "I haven't heard what my daughter has to say on national television."

"Mom—"

She raises her hand. "You don't say a word." She doesn't even look at me.

I want to cover my ears and run out of the apartment.

Uncle Miguel doesn't take his eyes off me. It's like shame replaced the blood in my body, and I feel it seep into every organ, every joint, every muscle.

"I'm sorry," I say. "This wasn't supposed to happen."

"Who posted it, then?" Raj asks. "If you didn't do it, who did?"

"Someone on the school paper. I don't know him as well as I thought I did."

How could he do this to me? I won't say it was Josh. I won't turn him in, but I won't trust him again. Ever.

"Charlotte," Mom says. I'm prepared for her to cry or even yell. I brace myself. "Go to your room. We'll discuss the situation and let you know how it will be handled. You're grounded. You are not to leave this apartment. You are not going for a run, you are not going down to the bakery. You are not going anywhere."

"And you will not speak to a member of the media, including the ace reporters on the school paper," Uncle Miguel says.

I look at each of them: Mom, Uncle Miguel, and Raj. The magnitude of my mistake is clear. Just this afternoon, I felt relieved knowing that I didn't have to deal with this alone. Yet here I am now. Exactly that. Entirely alone.

Twenty-Five

I delete Josh's texts without reading them.

I want to call Emma, hear her voice, tell her how right she was. But I worry that if Mom hears me on the phone, she'll take it away and forbid me from talking to anyone.

I stick to texting. Emma is kind and generous. She doesn't say, *I told you so.* Instead, she tells me that her acceptance letters arrived too.

We compare notes. She didn't get into USC or Northwestern either. Or Berkeley. She got into Brown, though, and I know that's her favorite.

We'll figure it out, we promise. There are bigger and more pressing issues at hand, like pissing off the FBI. Way to alienate the United States government.

I can't bring myself to read the news. If I see my face on TV, I'll destroy either the screen or my face. A toss-up.

Josh is persistent, but not more than me. I stop counting

the number of texts. I delete each one as soon as I see his name. I don't tell Emma this. Most of me feels betrayed, but part of me is still protective. I don't know why.

I wonder if this is how Mom feels right now, the way I feel about Josh. Confused and hurt and a particular kind of angry that I've never felt before.

I hear voices and the door and then quiet. I lie on the floor now, in the nest Emma and I made. I snuggle under the pile of down comforters, well aware that I'm in exile.

Mom finally opens my bedroom door. She seems hurt and exhausted, and she still won't look at me. "Give me your phone," she says.

"But, Mom—"

"Give it to me, Charlotte. *Teper'*. Now."

I place it into her hand. Now I have nothing to hold on to. I can't cradle Josh's cannonball rock. Not anymore. I should hurl it out the window, except with my luck, it'd strike an old lady shopping for produce at the Chinese market across the street.

"No more talking to anyone. You and your friends have done enough damage. Wait until tomorrow when Raj comes back. He wants to meet with us after they have an idea of the ramifications. I never thought you'd be so foolish. I'm going to bed. Get some sleep."

"Mom—"

"I don't want to discuss this. I'm going to bed. You should too."

She's made it clear that I can't leave the apartment or communicate with the outside world. Apparently, I can't leave my room either.

She turns off my lights.

I close my eyes, not because I expect to sleep, but because it is the only thing I can bring myself to do.

Twenty-Six

She's gone when I wake up. I smell apples and apricots. She's downstairs with Tatya Nadine, baking as she details my sins.

Dad's car keys are gone as well. She must think I'm a flight risk.

I want to shroud the TV in blankets. I can't even watch a movie. I can't stand the possibility of seeing my own face on the screen.

She's brewed coffee, so she doesn't completely hate me. Then again, she could have made it for Raj Singh and Uncle Miguel.

It's unfair to compare my captivity to Dad's, but I do. I wonder how he passes his time. Is he left alone for hours on end? Does he have anything to read? Aside from missing us, he must be going crazy knowing the Giants will start playing next month. He's stuck in Eastern Europe, where they probably don't give a shit about major league baseball.

I stretch like I'm going for a run.

I finish off the coffee.

I'm starving, but the kitchen is bare. I could go downstairs for breakfast. I'm sure that's what Mom's expecting, but I'm taking my imprisonment literally. Besides, shame still pumps through my veins.

Maybe I'll ransack Mom's room and search for my phone, though if she was cunning enough to take Dad's car keys, she's wise enough to keep my phone with her.

The college packets still sit on the coffee table, but I can't bring myself to think about my future when I've messed up the present so spectacularly. And publicly. So much for staying behind the camera.

I can't get Raj's words out of my head. The rebels may retaliate. They may hurt Dad for my stupid mistake. I imagine Dad sitting on that mattress, with triple the number of bruises blooming across his skin. A bloody face. Broken bones. If they hurt him, I'm responsible.

We have a 1,800-square-foot apartment. With the exception of my parents' bedroom, I walk every inch.

My room is a mess. I could clean it, but I don't want Mom to associate my grounding with anything positive. I'll take responsibility for the video—not its airing, but its existence— but not for improving the conditions of my room.

That's when I see it. She took my phone, but not my laptop.

The stairs squeak. The floor creaks. I'll hear her approach, but she was clear: no communication with the outside world. I shut my door and burrow in my nest of blankets, leaving on the overhead light so the glowing blue hue of the computer won't be so visible if she comes in unexpectedly.

My in-box contains 163 new messages, mostly from people I've never heard of before.

Emma sent a recap of college news: Isaac got into Columbia, Dartmouth, and Stanford. Not surprising, given his grades. She says she'll call my mom today, after things quiet down in the bakery, ask if she can visit. She doesn't mention Josh.

Four messages from him. I delete them all without opening them.

One from Megan. She spoke to Mom last night. She's worried and is available if I need anyone to talk to. Have I considered broadcast journalism? She thinks I'm a natural in front of the camera. I never took her for someone who would type smiley faces in emails, not with her tattoos and a dozen earrings. She goes on to tell me that she shared my photos with Mr. Donoghue, the ones I left drying in the darkroom. Since she imagines I might be absent from school next week, she is assigning me an independent project—to distract me and keep me focused on something positive, she says. Create a photo essay that draws from personal experience, but not from the current situation with my father. Something personally or culturally significant. Be abstract. Use metaphor. Don't rely on portraiture. Transcend yourself, she instructs. Whatever that's supposed to mean.

Exile *and* homework.

I slide the laptop under my bed to keep it hidden from Mom.

My pictures of the bread, the piece with Mom's message written on it, were different from anything I've ever taken. It wasn't just that they were of an object; I knew that they captured emotion. I'd managed to take a photo of my feelings. The depth. Everyone tells me I overthink, but there was something about that morning, how I was rushed for time, worried about being late. More than that, though, I had confidence. Mom believed in me. She wanted me. She loved me. These are things we're supposed to take for granted, but I never could—maybe never can—because of what happened with Lena. I'm the daughter who lived. That should put me in a winning position, but it doesn't. No one can compete with grief. My baby sister will never grow up and make the stupid move of filming a video that could be considered treason.

That's when it comes to me: the game I play with myself, how Mom is the ghost mother and I'm the *potercha,* the troubled spirit of a dead child. How we're characters in Russian folklore.

I pull the book off my shelf, the illustrated one Mom used to read to me when I was little. It doesn't take long to flip through the pages. I've always related to other stories, the ones about the Snow Maiden and the Firebird, but I haven't considered this one before. Two daughters. One good and one bad. One who leaves and one who stays.

Twenty-Seven

A stepmother lived with two daughters, one her own and one her husband's. Her love was unequal and cruel, just like in *Cinderella*. Every time she looked at her stepdaughter, she pictured her husband's past, his first wife—his first and true love. She died in childbirth. He never recovered, not really. He carried a visible sadness. His new wife had hoped she could make his sorrow go away, but no matter what she did, she couldn't bring him the same joy. Anger, at first as small as a stone, was born and grew with each passing year.

She blamed her stepdaughter, who was as beautiful and kind as her dead mother. The stepmother aimed all of her rage and resentment at the innocent girl, who grew up in a house of quiet fury.

The stepmother came up with a solution to her problem: banish her stepdaughter. If she couldn't have her husband's love, she could at least dispose of the girl.

Who knows how—magic or threats or intimidation—but the stepmother convinced her husband to abandon his child in the middle of the woods in the middle of the winter.

The father was a coward. His fear eclipsed love. He chose his wife over his own flesh and blood because he was too weak and too spineless to fight. As the stepmother watched, the father cried as he helped the girl, wearing a sheepskin, into the sleigh. Even though he wept as he drove to the field at the beginning of the woods, he still coaxed her out of the sleigh and left her there to die.

He was too ashamed to say good-bye. He didn't look back as he returned to the house.

The girl, alone and devastated and terrified, stood in the ankle-deep snow.

The woods and the surrounding field belonged to Father Frost. The old man, with his long white beard, radiant crown, and layers of thick furs, had been watching the poor daughter's fate. He didn't want to scare her, so he walked slowly from the woods to the center of the field.

"Do you know who I am?" he asked.

She nodded. "Hello, Father Frost. Thank you for sharing your field with me."

Father Frost, the King of Winter, was impressed by her gentle manners and kind heart. But he knew the girl wouldn't survive long in the cold. He offered her a trunk filled with everything that could keep her warm: beautiful silk quilts, furs, and more clothes than she ever could have imagined. Of all the dresses, one stood out, a deep blue *sarafan* embroidered with silver thread and embellished with pearls.

She slipped on the dress, and the woods quieted at her beauty.

In the meantime, the stepmother, confident that the girl had frozen to death within hours, prepared the traditional funeral dishes. She ordered her husband to go fetch his dead daughter's body and bring her back to be buried. The guests would come shortly.

Once more, the coward listened to his heartless wife and set off for the field.

The stepmother baked bread and made a rich stew before starting on cookies and a pie. From the kitchen window, she was astonished to see her husband and stepdaughter walk to the house. The girl was beautifully dressed and beaming with happiness. The father could barely carry the heavy trunk.

The woman rushed out, yelling at her husband to prepare the sleigh and drive her own daughter out to the field.

The husband obliged and abandoned his stepdaughter in the exact same spot.

Father Frost emerged from the woods again, assessing his new guest. "Do you know who I am?" he asked.

She practically growled as she told him to go away and leave her alone.

Father Frost tried again, seeing the girl's teeth rattle from the cold. She responded rudely to each of his kind questions. Father Frost grew angrier and angrier. What was wrong with this child? Finally, he gave up, leaving her to the snow.

Back at the house, the woman tossed out the funeral dishes and started to work on a celebratory meal. Soon, she was convinced, her daughter would return with an equally enormous fortune, if not an even bigger one. Perhaps a larger and heavier trunk.

She turned to her husband and commanded him to fetch her child. She set the table, plotting out her daughter's future, thinking of all the eligible bachelors in the village. She spotted the sleigh in the distance. She dried her hands and rushed to greet them. Her husband carried the frozen body of her daughter into the house. At last, the mother understood what she had done.

Twenty-Eight

By eleven o'clock, the fog appears to be growing thicker by the hour. I don't want to shoot in black and white. I need color, but the only way to achieve what I want, that over-saturated Technicolor effect, is to go digital. That means removing the darkroom from the process, something I have a hard time giving up. Then again, it's not like I'll have access to the darkroom in the immediate future.

I have a printer and plenty of photo paper. I have my camera and laptop. I have what I need to complete Megan's assignment.

Except for Mom's beaded rose gown, everything is in the attic. A rope dangles from the hallway ceiling. It takes a couple of tries for me to yank hard enough to release the ladder, something Dad easily does with one hand.

Our flat may be cluttered, but the attic is pristine and organized. Mom's trunks from Russia rest against neat stacks of crates and bins. I almost expect signage and labels. Grief does that, keeps things tidy. Up here, my parents preserve Lena through her belongings, some that were handed down to me.

I know what I need.

I empty one of Mom's trunks of blankets and the kind of winter coats one would never use in California. I keep the quilt and put everything else aside.

There's a bin full of clothes I never wore. Dresses for an infant, spanning the year in sizes. The nine- to twelve-month dresses still have their tags.

Pink and yellow and coral and peach. Layers of lace and frills. Those embroidered with gold thread were gifts from Russia, from aunties showering Mom with gifts.

I lay them one on top of the other, draping the dresses over the quilt, creating the illusion of Father Frost's gift.

I took Mom's gown but left her jewelry. That felt too private. Trespassing. Instead, I add Lena's toys: a stuffed bunny, a rattle. They start as substitutes, but they are treasures in their own right. When I'm done, the trunk brims with riches, and except for the quilt and gown, all belonged to Lena.

I blow through one roll, then two. By the time I have everything back in place, Mom hasn't come home yet. I've never felt so alone in the house.

I'm shooting out of order, putting Father Frost's gift

before the abandonment in the snow. I needed privacy in the attic, time to go through Lena's things. Mom wouldn't understand. The mere sight of me opening those bins would cause her pain. The attic isn't off-limits; it's just tucked away, always there but never opened. Dad ventures up for Christmas decorations, and other than that, the door remains closed.

When I was little, three or four, I thought Lena lived up there. I'd hear Mom crying through the ceiling. Sometimes, when she needed to be alone, she'd climb the ladder to be close to Lena's things.

In the kitchen, I pull out sugar and chunky gray salt and flour, dumping them on the butcher block. I empty the ice into the sink and bash it with a rolling pin, reducing cubes to crystals. This is how Mom finds me, a violent maniac with a rolling pin. I'm pink and flushed and sweating from the effort.

"What on earth are you doing?"

"Art project," I say. I'm covered in flour. I need a shower.

Mom surveys the kitchen, looking even unhappier with me. Like that's possible. "You're cleaning this up."

"I know."

"Now," she says. She's possessive about the kitchen. Territorial. I know better, but I didn't expect her home so early.

"Why aren't you at the bakery?"

She hands me a plate. Piroshki.

"Thanks. I'm starving," I say.

"I assumed you would come downstairs."

I shrug. "Enjoying my imprisonment, I guess."

"Don't act like this is some grave injustice, Charlotte. You have no idea of the consequences of that video. It put your father at risk. I can't believe you would be so *glupyy*." Foolish.

"The last thing I want to do is hurt him. I was trying to help. I told you I didn't post it!"

"No, but you made it in the first place. Without talking to me. Without talking to Miguel. The FBI is another matter, but you didn't come to us."

"I didn't plan for things to turn out this way. We came up with the idea and went for it. It seemed like it could help. You know we have to keep him in the news. We talked about that on Friday night."

"Yes, we talked about talking about it. You were never supposed to *do* anything." She yanks her hair free from her ponytail and shakes it out so it falls to her shoulders. She, too, is covered in flour.

"Someone had to do something, Mom." I try to hang on to my intention: to help Dad, even though now I worry that I've done more harm than good.

"If you had just waited. Uncle Miguel was going to keep

working on his publisher—he felt confident he could persuade the paper. I don't know why you couldn't just wait."

"Because I'm sick of waiting! Will Baxter's parents have been waiting for years. We all agree that can't happen to Dad. And, sorry, Mom, but it's not like you were going to do anything. I'm lucky that you're out of bed. I know you don't want to be stuck here with me, but you better get used to it. Dad may never come home. I know you wish it was Lena who had lived and not me."

If I had slapped her or set her on fire, I'm sure it would have hurt less.

I can't believe I spoke those words out loud, and as I watch her face fill with pain and tears spill onto her cheeks, regret blooms inside me. I'd do anything to take the words back. "Oh, Mom, I'm so sorry. I didn't mean that. Really." I take a step closer, but she moves out of reach.

I want her to yell or scream. Say anything. Punish me in some way. But Mom is silent, so completely still that she may have been made out of marble or plaster.

"I'm so sorry," I repeat.

She's standing before me, but she's gone. She's left me again.

Twenty-Nine

After the earthquake in Ukraine hit, buildings and roads and houses were reduced to rubble. Smoke and ash and destruction.

Somehow, in less than a day, I've managed to create similar conditions here.

I've never, not once, spoken to Mom—or anyone—like that. I regret it in every molecule of my body. I've never felt so ashamed, even when my face appeared on national television. It will take a lot to make up for what I've done. It's like I'm burning down the house and everything in it.

Mom opens my bedroom door. She's out of her baking clothes, wearing jeans and a T-shirt and sneakers. "Get dressed, Charlotte."

I don't ask where we're going. I obey and pull on the exact same clothes as her.

I follow her out of the apartment and into the garage. As

we drive through the city and across the Golden Gate Bridge, she doesn't say a word. Nothing but silence, a different kind than I'm used to. Mom's rarely angry at me. Not like this. It's as though she's expressing something I always feared was inside her—a fury for what I did to her body when I was born.

We park at Muir Beach. It's low tide, and the fog's so thick that I can't see the bridge and the Farallon Islands. I gaze into the ocean, at the wavering expanse of water, so large that it defies shape and containment. The other side of the ocean is irrelevant, the opposite shore meaningless.

"Dad used to bring me here," I say. "Remember? We'd come really early and hunt for sand dollars. I was what, three or four? In preschool."

"No," she says.

"I was older?"

"You're right about the age, but your father never took you here. That was me. You were so upset when your dad would leave that I'd take you outside. It was the only way to calm you down. We came here, even in the rain."

"But the sand dollars," I say. They still line my window-sill. "Why don't I remember that it was you?"

The wind whips her hair, and she struggles to put it in a ponytail. "I think we have a hard time seeing each other sometimes. Let's walk."

It's like we both took a vow of silence and the gulls

overhead are the only ones who speak, with their relentless caws. Mom leans over and presses a sand dollar into my hand. I trace the rough edge with my finger and the embossed flower in the center. Sand dollars have a season, just like tulips, just like peaches. This is a rare time of the year to stumble upon one. Mom taught me this. How could I have forgotten? What else have I forgotten?

We've walked a good distance down the beach when Mom bends over again. "Give me your hand."

I oblige. She places something sharp and cold in my palm. A shell, sandy, with a broken edge. The wide mouth tapers into a small curved top. "Scallop."

"Right," she says. "And here's another." A long half shell, narrow as a dragonfly's wing, smooth on the inside and rough lines on the outside. A mussel.

"We need to turn around if we're going to beat traffic," she says.

She bends down once more. "Your favorite."

Mom places an abalone shell in my hand, its shallow shape as distinct as the mottled rainbow colors inside. I have such an affinity for this shell with its muted eddy of color, abstracted circles—a perfect mirror of how I feel, so many emotions swirled together that I can't identify the primary one. I slip it into my pocket.

"This is what we used to do. All the time."

"Why did you bring me here today?" I ask.

She stops walking and looks at me. Tears gather at the edges of her eyes, but don't fall. "You never would have said that to me if you remembered our trips to the beach. I don't know how to make you understand how much I love you. You're my child. My *serdtse.*" Heart.

I wipe my cheeks dry. I wish I had the words to explain how I feel. I'll have to show her instead.

Thirty

I was raised not to waste, and even though my photo project has lost its magic, I return to the kitchen and sprinkle freshly broken ice crystals onto the sugar and flour.

It doesn't take long for me to recognize my power. I'm the storyteller. I don't have to create a literal interpretation of the folktale. I can make it my own.

There doesn't have to be one sister who stays and another who leaves. I don't have to damn the father to cowardice and the mother to menace. Sometimes things happen and no one is to blame.

I rework the scene, leaving the snow but changing the story. I'd removed the figurines from my old dollhouse in the attic, along with nesting dolls from my room, to use as characters. Now I place them in the snow and shoot. I rearrange the scene and shoot again. I don't have the confidence I did earlier, or the other day, but I'm too defeated to overthink anything.

By the time I finish and clean the kitchen, Mom still hasn't emerged from her room. I take out my laptop, not caring if she sees it and confiscates it. I want to work on the project. It's not homework anymore. It's for her.

The notes from the spring break camp help, and I follow the steps I learned in the digital photography class. I over-saturate the color and intensify the contrast. I don't want the dolls to resemble dolls, so I crop and use shadows. It works, but each step takes time. I don't want to be sloppy. I don't want to rush.

Sometimes words aren't enough. I know that's the case for Mom and me.

I need to do something to get her back.

Each picture takes about an hour, but I become faster as I go, shaving off time. Not that I expect to sleep, with everything that's going on.

As I tinkered with the makeshift snow, I rewrote the folk-tale by hand, and now, as I type it up, I make a few changes here and there. Now the parents are married and always have been. They are kind and loving, but the mother can't keep the father home. He works too much. He's curious. He likes to explore.

They have two daughters, one just like the mother and one just like the father. The oldest girl, the one who takes after her dad, enjoys exploring too. As soon as she learns to

walk, she ventures outside, going farther and farther, instill-
ing panic in her parents. They give the girl a sister, hoping
that will keep her home. But their older daughter is restless,
even more than her father, and one day she skips outside to
play and never comes back.

The younger daughter is a taller, darker version of her
quiet and domestic mother. She likes adventure and explo-
ration in small doses only. After her sister disappears, the
house fills with cold. Whenever the wind blows, the fire and
candles go out. No matter how hard her mother tries, the
house remains dark.

One day when they expect the father to return from a
trip, they receive a letter. He's delayed. The mother has been
cooking for hours, and they're nearly out of firewood. "Go to
the forest," she tells her daughter. "Fetch some wood."

The girl wraps herself up in a thick blanket and pulls
the sleigh through the ankle-deep snow to the edge of the
woods. She's met by an old man dressed in white.

"Do you know who I am, child?"

"You're Father Frost," she says. "May I take some wood?
Our house is so cold."

Father Frost, the King of Winter, knows the girl won't
survive long in the cold. He offers her a trunk filled with
everything that will keep her warm: beautiful silk quilts, furs,
and more clothes than she ever could have imagined. Of all

the dresses, one stands out: a deep blue *sarafan* embroidered with silver thread and embellished with pearls.

She slips on the dress and the woods quiet at her beauty.

He waves his hand, and the girl sees that the sleigh is stocked high with not only wood.

The girl hears a familiar voice and watches as her long-vanished sister approaches her. She hasn't aged a day since she left three years earlier.

"Hello, sister. Please don't tell Mama and Papa that I'm here. They'll see my things in the trunk. I put in some toys and the dress I wore the day I left. I can stay a child with Father Frost. I never have to grow up. Please don't make me go back. Tell them I'm safe and happy. Tell Mama not to be sad. Tell Papa to stay at home. Tell them to take good care of you."

Father Frost looks at the girl. "Can you do that?"

The girl stares at her sister, seeing her happiness and contentment. It would be cruel to bring her home when she so clearly belongs with Father Frost.

The girl nods, sad that she has to leave her sister, but happy knowing she's safe. She belongs in the woods. There, she is free.

Thirty-One

I work through the night, and when I finish the project very early in the morning, I print two copies—one for Megan and one for Mom. I leave Mom's on the counter by the coffeepot, where I know she'll see it first thing.

It's easy to leave the apartment unnoticed and walk to the bus stop in the chilly fog. The noises of the bakery drown out my footsteps. It's early enough that I should be able to catch Megan before anyone else is there. I need to turn this in. I need to see how she reacts to the photos. I can't make a decision without that.

I elbow my way onto the crowded bus. Hands overlap as we all cling to the rail, trying to ride the lurches like they're waves. I don't plan to stay at school once I turn in my work—can't deal with everyone's stares and whispers. I can't see Josh right now. I'm too hurt. Too angry. And I honestly can't deal with one more thing.

I arrive to the smell of coffee, which means it's already later than I'd hoped. Megan looks surprised to see me. Before she can say anything, I blurt out, "I just wanted to drop this off. I'm not staying." I hand her the folder.

She pours me a mug of coffee. "How are you holding up? Have you heard anything about your dad since your video came out?"

I shake my head. "I'm worried that it backfired. The FBI said it could make things worse for him. The rebels might hurt him as a way to retaliate."

"Oh, Charlotte. I'm so sorry. I'm here if you need someone to talk to."

"Thanks."

Megan takes out the photos one at a time. "God, the color."

I watch as she spreads them out in order and reads the accompanying story. She goes back to the trunk shots, holding one up to the light. Lena's rattle rests in a nest of lace dresses.

"Sit," she says.

I'd been hovering.

"Charlotte, who knows what kind of photographer you'll end up being. Journalistic. Portrait. Fine art. There's no telling. But you could do any and all of them. Emma said you got into Berkeley and State and Emerson?"

"And NYU," I say. "But I've always wanted to stay close to home. I still do. The thing is, though, I don't really feel ready for school. Maybe that'll change if my dad comes home, but right now, I don't want anything to do with journalism. I can say this for sure: I don't want to be a photojournalist. Not anymore."

"This isn't about out earlier conversation, is it? Because I never meant to give you the impression that you aren't talented. You *are*. If anything, you have so much talent that I think it would be good for you to explore all forms of photography. Explore everything. That's what college is about."

I shake my head. "No, I've been thinking about this for a while. My dad loves that I work on the paper. And my best friends are just like him. But I'm not. To be honest, I never have been, and I'm just seeing that now, you know, really seeing it. I can't keep doing something because I'm trying to be something or someone else. I'm happier spending an entire day taking pictures of a slice of bread than shooting an assembly or science fair." I take a deep breath before making my announcement. "I want off the paper. I'm even thinking of taking a year off from school. I might decline admittance to all of them."

Megan practically spits out her coffee. "Charlotte, I've tried my best to be supportive and not bossy, but under no circumstances can you turn down college. Do you have any idea how hard it is to get into those schools?"

"But I told them this story of me following in my dad's footsteps. It was a love letter to the media. That's not what I want to do now. That's not who I am."

She laughs gently. "Guess how many majors I had."

"I don't know. Two?"

"Four. I started out as premed. If my parents can adjust their expectations, so can yours. My undergraduate degree is from Johns Hopkins. I didn't go there to study international relations. Promise me you'll accept Berkeley. It's your top choice, and they have a great art department. You'll do well there. And you came back from camp saying you didn't want to go to college anywhere else."

"I know it's late in the year, but can I drop the paper and move to Mr. Donoghue's class? Is that even possible?"

"We'll make it work. I support your decision to take a break from the paper, especially given what your family is going through."

I barely manage a smile. "Thank you. I need to leave before the bell."

"You'd better get going, then." Megan picks up a photo. "This is great work. I can't believe you did it in a day."

"I'm grounded, so I don't have much else to do. It helped, though. Being in the darkroom always calms me, but working like this did, too."

"Keep taking pictures, Charlotte. You have a point of view. That's important and rare."

I nod and thank her again. "I will," I say. "I promise."

Thirty-Two

I listen to Dad's beloved Cuban hip-hop as I wait for the bus home. I don't understand Spanish, but I looked up the lyrics online. All love songs, unrequited and pining and passionate. One in particular is so explicit that I blush whenever I hear it.

I take a few steps toward the curb and nearly walk right into him. Josh, wearing a hooded sweatshirt and jeans and black combat boots. If I hadn't studied him so closely for years, the precise way he puts one foot in front of the other, I wouldn't have known him through the thick fog.

"Jesus, Josh," I say. "You scared the crap out of me."

He pushes back his hood and looks as wrecked as I feel. For a second, I forget that I'm not speaking to him.

He meets my eyes and reaches for my hand, and even though I've spent every hour of the past year wanting him to touch me, now all I feel is the cold. And my anger. I pull away.

"You know, I don't like talking trash about people, but

you need to know that I didn't do this. I'd *never* do that to you. It's your video and it's your story and he's your dad. I'd never post that unless you asked me to. Ever. And if you don't believe me, then I guess you really don't know anything about me. And that fucking sucks because I thought if anyone got me, it was you."

"You took the video, Josh. It was on your phone. What, am I supposed to believe Emma's parents have a nanny-cam or something and someone hacked and posted it?"

Josh hands me his phone with the videos loaded. "Just watch."

"I don't want to see this again. I know what I said."

"Just watch, Charlotte. Please."

"Fine." I press play and see my face on the screen. I want to look away or close my eyes or kick him, but then I see it. His thumb totally obscuring the recording for a few seconds. It's not the same one that was posted. He couldn't have edited it out. I was midsentence.

"If it wasn't you, who?"

He doesn't look at me. Instead, he unzips his backpack and shoves his bike helmet in. "There were two other people in the room, Charlotte. I told you that you could trust me."

He doesn't wait for me to respond before he turns and disappears into the fog.

Thirty-Three

I open the door to find Mom at the kitchen table, waiting.

"You left," she says.

"I had to take something to school. I caught the bus."

She meets my eyes. "You're grounded. You didn't tell me where you were going. Please don't do that again."

"Mom," I say. "I'm sorry. I'm so sorry."

She glances down at the photos. Unlike Megan's, hers aren't spread out. Instead, they're stacked neatly, as though she plans to bind them into a book. "You've been wanting to say that to me for years."

"Which part? The folktale?"

"Lena. That you thought I only loved Lena. Or loved her more."

If I told her the truth, that she's right, I'm not sure who I would hurt more: her or me.

"After the stroke, I couldn't move the left side of my body.

I couldn't nurse you properly. I couldn't hold you for more than a little while. I couldn't speak. Your father did a wonderful job feeding you and getting you to sleep. It was like you knew our limits. You cried, but not like Lena. Never too much.

"When I was strong enough to hold you, I kept getting out of bed just to make sure you were breathing. I barely slept, which made me take longer to recover. Finally, we had a routine. We both could sleep longer than four-hour stretches. Your father worked the city desk so he didn't have to travel. I got stronger. You grew. Then a tsunami hit Japan, and your dad volunteered to go. Miguel told him no. He had to stay home. We needed him here. But your dad had to go. He didn't know how to sit back and let someone else report that story. I don't think it was ego. He really wanted to help people. He went over Miguel's head. It took them a while to repair that."

Mom drains the rest of her coffee and rises to get more. "Do you want some?"

"Sure," I say. "Thanks."

"I didn't sleep again once your dad left. I got up over and over to see if you were okay. Finally, I brought you to bed with me, but I still couldn't sleep. Your dad was gone for nine days. I probably managed an hour or two a night.

"He started traveling more. I slept less. It wasn't that I

221

loved you less. I loved you so much. I loved you entirely. But I couldn't contain the fear of losing you. I don't think you're a *potercha* or a ghost. I think you're a child, a fragile child, and anything can happen to you. If I had my way, I would have slept next to you every night. I would have walked you to school and stayed all day. I had to learn how to give you space. To let you do some things on your own. I had to learn how to let you be a child. In doing that, I created this *rass-toyaniye.*" Distance. "And it grew and grew. And I've been too scared to live any other way. Do you understand what I'm trying to say?"

I wipe my cheeks with the back of my hand. "Yes," I whisper. "I think so."

"This, though." Mom picks up the photos. "This makes me think you understand. How did you come up with this?"

"That book you used to read from. Sometimes I pretend we're different characters from it. This time, I decided to change the story. The original doesn't really fit us."

"No, not as it's written in the book." She taps the pictures. "You made it into a better story. The family has choices. They can choose to let go. They can choose to take care of each other. I choose you, Charlotte. No matter what happens with your dad, I won't disappear again. I'm your mother. I'm here. I want you to stay home too. Stay close."

"I want to go to Berkeley," I say.

"You always have." She smiles like she did when we celebrated the day of the Renaissance Faire. A real smile that makes her look young and strong. She's smiling for me. Because of me. "And I'm so glad you're choosing home."

Mom and I walk to the couch, and she pulls me close, like I'm a baby, like I'm still that preschooler she took to Muir Beach. Spooned together on the couch, we finally sleep.

Thirty-Four

The first thing Mom says when we wake is that I'm still grounded. No more leaving.

"Here," she says as she hands me my phone. "You can talk to your friends, except the one who leaked the video. We'll talk more about that later. I need to go downstairs and help Nadine."

She pulls me close and gives me a lingering hug. "You're everything to me, Charlotte."

I hold on tight. She releases me with a kiss on my forehead.

As soon as my phone's powered on, it rings in my hand as if on command. It's Emma.

"Finally! I've needed to talk to you for days and you're not answering your email. It wasn't Josh, Charlotte. He didn't post the video. Isaac did, and he feels terrible. He thought he was helping."

Relief and rage both hit me at once.

Relief that it definitely wasn't Josh, even though I believed him this morning. Relief that it wasn't Emma, because I can't live without her, and losing her would crush me as much as losing Dad.

Isaac. I love Isaac. How could he do this?

I squeeze my eyes shut. I'm feeling too many things at once, and I'm desperate for a moment of calm. I want to set everything aside, my head and my heart and every sense and feeling they produce, and stick them in one of the trunks upstairs.

I return to my nest and bury myself under the blankets, trying to create some comfort.

"He knew what he was doing, Em. This is Isaac. He's a savant when it comes to the news. He could have run CNN when he was twelve. I'm sure he really thought he was helping. I think he knew that none of us would post it. The paper wouldn't let Miguel. The FBI wouldn't let the paper. If he did it, then it could happen without getting anyone in too much trouble."

I let out a bitter laugh. "Except I'm in a world of trouble and a world of pain. The whole thing might have made it worse for my dad. And I blamed Josh. I ghosted him. Was that part of the plan? To throw Josh under the bus?"

"No! That's what made Isaac tell. He realized that you

were getting blamed and then that Josh was. He went to Megan and he called Miguel and he's going to call your mom."

"He shouldn't bother," I say, knowing it won't make a difference. Nothing can fix what I've done by making the video in the first place. "He should leave my mom alone."

"I'm going to be late for class. But can I come over later?" Emma asks.

I'd love nothing more than to hide in my room with Emma, but I need to fix things with Josh. Plus, I'm pretty sure no contact with the outside world means hanging out with Emma is forbidden.

"I'm still grounded."

"But she'd let me come over, right? You're grounded, sure, but not *that* grounded."

I let out a long sigh. "If Uncle Miguel could have grounded me, he would have. You should have seen Raj Singh. Boy Wonder was about to lose it. We've created a shit show."

Emma laughs. "I need to meet this Raj Singh."

"Will you do me a favor? Give me half an hour and then find Josh and tell him to check his email, okay?"

"Sure," she says. "What about Isaac?"

"I can't deal with him right now. I'm too upset, and I already said things to my mom that I regret. The damage is done. The FBI and my mom say we put my dad in danger."

"What do you mean?"

"They're worried that the video might make the rebels retaliate. I feel so awful, Em. What if this hurt him? I can't stop thinking about it."

"Oh my God. I'm sorry. Damn Isaac."

I sigh into the phone. "I know. We all thought it was a good plan."

"When will you be back at school?" she asks.

"I'm not sure—probably not this week."

"Seriously?" Emma asks.

"Yeah. It's that big of a deal." I close my eyes and rub my temples, trying to stop the building headache.

"You'll tell me when you're allowed to see people?"

"Yeah," I say. "Promise."

"I'm really sorry, Charlotte."

"Thanks. I am too. We never meant to hurt anyone."

"Of course not. But at least it worked. You've seen all the coverage, right?"

My eyes pop open. "What are you talking about?"

"Charlotte, the story is everywhere. Your dad is in every paper in the country. AP did a huge article."

I feel a hint of relief. At least we accomplished that. Dad hasn't been forgotten—for now. "I'll call when I can, okay?"

"I'm here. I'm here if you need me. Just say the word. We miss you. All of us."

"Thanks," I say. "I wish you were here. And go ahead and call whenever you want. Maybe my mom will break down and let you come over. She has a hard time saying no to you."

"I'll work on it," she says.

Thirty-Five

School let out an hour ago. My email to Josh was short and to the point: *I was wrong. Forgive me.*

Someone knocks at the front door. Probably Raj, here to tell me the many ways I thwarted the FBI's efforts and put my father in even worse danger.

I open the door to Josh. I still have flour in my hair and under my nails from my project, and I'm certain I smell. I can't remember the last time I showered. But he smiles at me like I hadn't treated him like the enemy.

"I'm sorry," I say. "I should've trusted you."

"I would have done the same thing if I were you."

I shake my head. "I don't think you would have."

"You're probably right. Get your stuff."

"I can't, Josh. I'm not allowed to leave and you can't stay. I'm in so much trouble."

"No, it's okay," he says. "I went to the bakery first and

talked to your mom. She's really nice. You look like her. Nadine is nice too."

"You did what?"

"You have permission to go out for an hour." He holds up a bag. "She even gave me pastries. Does she give all of your friends snacks, or does this mean she likes me?"

"She gives everyone snacks. She can't help herself. It's a compulsion."

"Glad to hear I'm so special. Get your coat. It's cold."

We climb into an ancient Honda, and when I accuse him of stealing it, he laughs and explains it belongs to his brother. Josh hates driving and considers cars nothing but convenient vehicles of death, but he knows I don't own a bike. We drive through Golden Gate Park, inching through the traffic, and snake up Twin Peaks. The fog is so thick, I can barely see the lights below. My camera will be of little use.

We park as close as we can get to Sutro Tower. He's right about the cold. I wrap my scarf tight and shove my hands into my pockets. It's nearly sunset and the wind is so strong, it whips right through our clothes.

"I'm really sorry," I say again. "I need you to know that. I never should have assumed it was you who posted it. I don't know why I did."

"Your friends don't like me, and it was one of your best

friends who posted it. I get it." He stares at his boots. He says it's okay, but I see that it's anything but.

"You didn't do anything to make me doubt you. I messed up. I jumped to conclusions. I was wrong. I did the same thing with my mom. I'm sorry."

I reach for his hand, and he meets my eyes. "Okay. I accept. Thanks. For the record, I never would have done that. It was a dick move. Isaac should feel bad."

I shake my head. "Isaac is the last person I need to worry about."

We follow the dirt path to the tower and sit at the base. "It's amazing on a clear night."

My eyes follow the skyline. Without the fog, you could probably see half the city. "I bet."

Josh hands me the bag of pastries. Turnovers. That means she likes him. I hand him one.

"We had our first fight, and we're still good, right? Major milestone," he says between bites. "Damn, your mom can bake."

"Right," I say. "That's very good."

When he kisses me, I wonder when touching him will seem common. Everything still feels so new. I lean against him, and he wraps his arms around me. I need the warmth. I need him. "Did you get your college letters?"

"Yeah. I got in to two out of my three. UCLA rejected

me, but I expected that. Solid SAT scores but mediocre grades. Good enough for San Francisco and San Jose State, though."

"So you'll be staying here. You're not going off to Princeton or something?"

"I'll be here, rooming with Ian and going to San Francisco State. They have a film department. When you were mad at me—and no matter what your friends say, I think Isaac set me up—I thought about turning down school altogether and riding my bike to L.A. and interning somewhere."

"You don't want to go to L.A. now? Can you do film here?"

"Coppola's here. DreamWorks and Pixar are here. George Lucas is here. San Francisco has a ton of film festivals and less competition than L.A. And a degree helps. I'd be an idiot to pass up this opportunity. Plus, my parents would kill me, and despite my reputation, I really don't want to make them unhappy. And now I know you're staying. I've never seen someone fit in as well as you did at Berkeley."

"You did too."

"I only took that camp because you did. I never would have spent spring break in school otherwise."

I pull away so I can look at him. "Why didn't you ever say anything? We could have been together a year or two ago."

He kisses me. "Why didn't *you* say something?"

He laughs when I roll my eyes. I fill him in on my other acceptances and rejections, tell him how Emma and I always wanted to go to college together, but now it looks like we won't. "And you should know that I'm off the paper. I'm not going to study journalism."

"What? You love the paper. Why would you quit?"

"I talked to Megan about all of this. I'm going to try more artistic photography, maybe study fine arts. So I'm dropping the paper and taking Mr. Donoghue's studio class instead."

"Can I transfer too? Because it's taking everything I have to resist kicking Isaac's ass, and if I get a third suspension, San Francisco State will rescind their offer of acceptance."

"Will you tell me why you got suspended the second time?" I ask.

"I would, but I can't." The smile fades from his face. "I did something to protect someone, and I promised I wouldn't tell. Plus, that could get me suspended again. Will you understand if I can't tell you?"

I think of how I'd been asked to keep secrets, and what happened when I broke that promise, even if it was to Raj Singh. "Yeah. Of course." I look up. "I think Sutro is a great name for your production company, by the way."

"I love it here. It's my favorite place. How about you?"

"Lands End. The windmill and the tulip garden, too,

because they're my dad's favorites." I close my eyes for a second and take in a breath. I can't imagine a life without Dad or walking through the park and sitting in the garden on my own or just with Mom. I can't exist in the city without him. "There's no way I'm going to college if he doesn't come home."

"I checked before I came to get you. The video is still on the news. It's still a lead story. There's no way the FBI isn't doing everything possible. It's probably their number one priority. I know we messed everything up by making the video, but I still think it was the right thing to do. Charlotte, you kind of own the Internet right now."

He shows me his phone, all his social media accounts. Dad is one of the top trending stories.

"We did it," I say, trying to hold on to the hope I had when we first decided to make the video. Back when I thought maybe, just maybe, my voice would be enough to bring Dad home. But that was before I understood the full repercussions of our actions. I have to swallow tears in order to speak. "Let's hope it works."

"I have a feeling it will," he says. "I know Isaac screwed everything up, but it's kind of great that we did this on our own. Made the video. We all did that together. *You* did that. I think that's something to be proud of, even though it didn't happen the way we all wanted. Except for Isaac."

"Yeah," I say, "it's much better to have actually done something than to be helpless. But I am grounded. Speaking of which, you need to keep your promise to my mother and get me back home. I'm in enough trouble as it is."

He stands and holds out his hand. "I'm happy to be in trouble with you."

Thirty-Six

I find Mom in the kitchen heating up take-out leftovers. "Right on time," she says. "I like your boyfriend."

"He's not my boyfriend," I say.

She raises an eyebrow. "Hmm, he said he is." She gives me her lopsided smile.

I can't help but smile back, and I feel light in a way I haven't in ages. Mom laughs at me. "I guess he is, then."

"It was nice to finally meet him. Has Emma come around, or is she still giving you grief over him?"

"You knew?" I ask. Emma and I try to be quiet, especially when it comes to discussing boys. God, what else does she know?

"You've been mooning over him for years. Of course I knew. Why don't you clear off the coffee table and see if you can find a good movie?"

Mom prefers aliens and spaceships to romantic comedies

because she grew up watching bootleg *Star Wars* videos, and that got her hooked. She finds dramas depressing and comedies are fine, depending on the cast. She's as finicky about film as she is about food. She and Josh will get along well. I settle on something we saw at the Kabuki a couple of years ago, one she loved and I'd happily watch again. I'll do anything to make her feel good—anything.

After we eat the mu shu, I curl up next to Mom and almost fall asleep. She strokes my hair. This is what it must feel like to be a cat, to want nothing more than food and affection and sleep.

We both startle at the knock at the door, hard and insistent.

Uncle Miguel rushes through as soon as Mom opens it. We need to make him a key.

He raises both hands in the air. A surrender. "Raj here wouldn't tell me what the news is, but I wore him down enough to know that it's good."

Mom jumps up but doesn't speak, too scared to even guess. I stand, too, but my legs feel wobbly. I realize I'm shaking. This is the moment we've been waiting for. Finally, news about Dad. Now I'm almost too terrified to listen.

I look at Uncle Miguel's broad smile and at Raj, who is practically giddy. "We have him! He's safe! We'll get you two on a plane to Germany first thing in the morning. You can meet him at the base there. He'll need to see a doctor and have a full debriefing."

"A doctor?" I ask. "What's wrong with him?" Mom wipes the tears off my cheeks. I didn't even realize I was crying. I'm still too worried to absorb the news.

"It sounds like he may have a couple of cracked or broken ribs. Otherwise, he's okay."

Mom pulls me toward her and wraps her arms around me. Uncle Miguel hoots and bear hugs us both. Dad is safe. No one's pointing a gun to his head. He's out of that terrible room with the small, filthy mattress. He's free. We'll see him tomorrow. I take a deep breath and allow myself to feel the relief.

"How'd you get him out?" I ask. More than anything, I want reassurance that I didn't make things worse with the video. That I'm not responsible for his broken ribs.

"Let's sit," Raj says.

Mom stacks our dinner plates and picks up a blanket and some stray pillows.

"Charlotte," Raj says, "I don't want to condone what you did. It could have had dangerous ramifications. Your father could have been hurt even more. He could have been *killed*. What you did was stupid. Really, really risky. But it worked. Broadcasting it in Russian brought in some good tips and leads. We probably would have found your dad, but this definitely made it happen sooner. Still, don't do anything like that again."

I may be hallucinating from all of the anxiety of the past few weeks, but I think Raj Singh just winked at me when he said that.

"What about Will Baxter?" I ask.

"These guys didn't have him," Raj says. "Another group does. We've never been able to pinpoint his location. It was easier with your dad. Most of the roads leading in and out of the village were destroyed, so we knew they had to be within a certain radius. Then the tips came in. Your dad was the only remaining hostage. His abduction was more opportunistic. Will Baxter's situation is different. They were watching him. They chose him."

We're all crying, me and Mom and Uncle Miguel. I can't help but feel sorrow for Will Baxter's family. I'm so relieved about Dad, and so sorry for them.

"I'll be back at seven tomorrow morning," Raj says. "Pack clothes for Jeremiah, too."

"I have a story to write," Uncle Miguel says. "Remember, I get the exclusive interview with the family. Don't go talking to other reporters or posting your own video, okay?" He hugs us again.

"Deal," I say.

"He's safe," Mom says after they've both gone. Her voice

is soft and filled with relief. She can't stop smiling, which only makes me smile more. She squeezes my hand.

"He is." I'm going to have my family back together, and we have the chance to be whole. The three of us. Not two—just me and Mom, with Dad missing. Not four, with the ghost of baby Lena filling the apartment. Three never felt like a complete number before. Now that it does, I can't stand the idea of us being apart. I look at Mom, knowing that she's with me for good. Dad might be free, but can he give up his dangerous stories? "Do you think he'll still want to travel so much?" I ask.

She thinks for a moment. "Not for a while. We'll keep him here for as long as we can, especially if Miguel can assign him something more interesting than the city council. But we've never been enough to keep him home. I've accepted this about your father. It's who he is. He loves us, though. More than anything."

"I know."

She kisses the top of my head. "And so do I."

I hug her tight. When she pulls away, she looks serious again.

"After we get your father, let's go to St. Petersburg. I want to show you where I grew up and where the folktales come from. It's springtime."

"The White Nights," I say.

"Well, it's too early for that, but the three of us can take a boat ride on the river. There's so much I want you to see. It finally feels like the right time. I know you'll miss more school, but under the circumstances, I think it will be fine. She tries to smooth my curls, an impossible task. "What do you think? Want to take a family vacation? We can stay with my sister. Tatya Rayna will be so happy to see us."

My eyes fill with tears. It's hard not to feel overwhelmed by all of this. My heart is having a hard time catching up. Mom's birthplace, home to the Snow Maiden and the Firebird. "I'd love that. Do you think Dad will want to come straight home, though?" It's hard to imagine how he'll feel until we see him. I can't believe that will be tomorrow.

Mom laughs. "Your father would never pass up a trip to St. Petersburg. He loves that city more than I ever did. My family will take good care of us."

When I hear the knock at the door, I'm worried it's Raj with bad news. Something went wrong. An ambush, or maybe Dad's injuries are worse than they thought. My muscles tense, and that familiar jolt of anxiety runs through me.

"It's probably Miguel." But when Mom opens the door, it's not him. "Josh, you're back."

He steps in looking unusually bashful, which is adorable. Just yesterday, I felt crushed by loss, and it was hard to find a hint of hope. And here we are now.

"Sorry to interrupt, but, Charlotte, I need to talk to you."

"You're not interrupting," I say, barely able to contain my smile. "They found my dad!"

I rush to him, and everything feels right as soon as his arms circle my waist. I hear the thump of his heartbeat before he whispers in my ear. "We did it, didn't we?"

I pull away, and he's smiling as big and goofy as I am. "Yes. Turns out we didn't get him killed after all." I look at Mom. "Is it okay if we take a walk?"

She smiles. "Yes, you're officially no longer grounded. But be back in an hour because we need to pack."

It's late, much later than I realized, and the fog is gone. A clear sky greets us. The stars, dimmed by the city lights, shine faintly from above. Josh takes my hand and leads me toward Golden Gate Park. We weave through hungry-looking people waiting for tables at the cluster of neighborhood restaurants. An elderly neighbor carries a bag of persimmons. The streets grow less crowded the closer we get to the park.

"I wasn't exactly being fair to you," he says.

"What do you mean?"

He slows his insanely fast pace. If I wasn't a runner, I'd be winded from trying to keep up. "I asked you to trust me, and you did until Isaac messed everything up. But I don't blame you for that. The point is, you did trust me with something super sensitive. I owe you the same."

The weathered pine trees welcome us, and we walk past the giant ferns with curling tendrils that always remind me of a Dr. Seuss illustration. He points to the left, and we plop down on the lawn in front of the Conservatory of Flowers, even more magnificent at night.

"Okay," I say. We sit cross-legged and facing each other. I take his hand.

"Do you remember that girl Hailey, the one who transferred over the summer?"

"Yeah, blondish hair, small, played volleyball. She was in our sophomore English class."

"That's her. A couple of girls on the team were taking pictures of her in the locker room, you know, while she was changing. They started texting them around. They never posted them, but they were going to."

"How do you know?"

"They told Hailey. I ran into her after school. She'd just left practice. She was losing it. She couldn't stop crying. I asked her who did it. At first, she wouldn't tell me, but she finally did. She refused to tell the coach. I broke into their lockers, which is a great skill to have, by the way. I took both girls' phones. One of them had her laptop. I took that, too."

"What did you do with them?"

"Hailey and I went to the beach. We threw them onto the

Great Highway and drove over them until they were totally smashed to bits."

"And you took the blame," I say. I didn't think it was possible to like him more, yet my heart swells.

"Well, I was the one who stole them. It was my idea. I do that: come up with ideas that get other people in trouble. I don't mean to, though. I'm trying to help. I did stop those girls."

"Why didn't everyone know? Seems like this would have gotten around."

He pauses a second and squeezes my hand. "In a few of the pictures, Hailey was completely naked. That's a felony. So none of us are supposed to talk about it. Hailey's parents had her on the waiting list at one of the private schools, and they managed to get her transferred. The other two girls are still here, but they were kicked off the volleyball team. They got in really big trouble. And I was suspended for two weeks for theft and vandalism. No charges. Now you know. I should have told you earlier."

I kiss his left cheek first, and then the other, before meeting his lips. "You did the right thing," I say.

"By telling you?"

"Yes, but also by destroying their stuff. You saved Hailey."

"That was the goal." He takes my other hand, and we form a circle. An electrical current could pass through us.

"I'm going to be gone for a little while. I'm not sure when I'll be back. A week or two probably." I tell him about Germany and St. Petersburg and boating down the Neva River.

He smiles at me, and I feel like I'm the only thought in his head. It's a beautiful, wonderful thing, to feel wanted and loved. I kiss him again.

"I'll be right here."

Acknowledgments

First, my deepest thanks to my agent, Faye Bender. Thank you for being my champion, partner, and dream maker. I consider myself the luckiest author in the world. I can't quantify my gratitude and fondness.

I am so fortunate to have found a home with Atheneum. Thanks to my brilliant editor, Reka Simonsen, who not only understands exactly what I'm trying to accomplish in a novel, but has the wisdom to push me a step farther. It's been a wonderful journey. Thanks to the amazing Simon & Schuster team, especially Michael McCartney, Clare McGlade, Aubrey Churchward, Audrey Gibbons, Katy Hershberger, Emily Hutton, Michelle Leo, Emma Ledbetter, Julia McCarthy, and Justin Chanda. To Wendy Sheanin, friend and fellow Californian-in-exile, a million thanks.

To my writing group: Jennifer Wilson, Catherine Knepper, Kali VanBaale, and Yasmina Madden. You make me a better writer and a better friend and Iowan.

To my family, especially my daughters, Lulu and Tillie. This book is for you. I'm so proud to be your mom. My sister Robyn, for believing in me. The Yenters and the Rongerudes for endless encouragement, especially Amy and Ben.

Kelsey Crowe, Mike Brown, and Georgia Brown, thank you for being my home away from home. Kelsey, you are my soul sister and I'm so glad we can share this journey as authors. To Pearl Piatt, Glen Price, and Abbey Piatt Price for decades of friendship. Abbey, your writing music kept me inspired for hours on end. To Amy Tang and Gabe Jenkins, I'd donate an organ to live in the same neighborhood again. Our autumn weekends mean so much. To cherished friend and reader Holly Herndon, thank you for the support and visits.

To friends Stacey Murphy, Brenda Tucker, Reena Krishna, Andrea DeLara, and Michael and Denise Tutty: thanks for the calls and visits and meals. They sustain me. MAPsters, I don't ever want to work with anyone else. Thank you for being such wonderful colleagues.

To the booksellers, bloggers, teachers, and librarians— champions and heroes—thank you for sharing my book with teen readers. Everyone has a story inside them and I'm so grateful to share mine.